MW01146308

Signed Books and more
www.mattshawpublications.co.uk

How Much 2

Book II

Matt Shaw

Enjoy the sickness!

PROLOGUE

Nate Stephenson walked into his manager's office and took a seat as instructed. His manager, Sharon Devlin, was sitting opposite him. The expression on her face did not suggest she was pleased to see him. Rightly so, Nate looked apprehensive. He knew what this was about.

Low viewing figures.

'Thank you for coming to see me at such short notice,' Sharon said in a very matter of fact tone. Despite there being a *thank you*, there was no hint of actual pleasantries with the way she addressed him.

Nate just smiled in response as he shifted uncomfortably in his seat.

'Do you know why I called you in?'

Nate shook his head.

'How long have you been here now?'

'About a month.'

'Steven showed you the ropes, didn't he?'

'Left me detailed instructions and we ran a session together.'

'I remember it. I also remember the viewing figures.' She added, 'We made a lot of money with that little game.'

'That's good.'

'Know what would be better?'

Nate knew it was a rhetorical question so stayed silent.

'What would be better,' Sharon explained, 'is if you didn't come along and think you could fuck with the format.'

Nate squirmed in his seat. He knew it had been a gamble but he had wanted to try something new to prevent the viewers from getting bored. He should have listened when Steven had explained how *they* don't like change. He had figured Steven had meant the audience watching the shows, not the management.

'We have a big following and your predecessor was making it bigger with each show he put on.' She asked, 'Do you read the comments on the uploads?'

'I don't.'

'You should. Then you might have seen just how badly you actually fucked things up with your… Whatever the fuck that was.' She paused a moment. 'Did you watch it?'

'Watch it?'

'What you produced.'

'I didn't.'

'It shows. Maybe if you had watched it, you wouldn't have released it. You would have come in here and asked for more time to prepare things.'

'Can I say something?'

'Of course.'

'I was trying something new…'

'Even though the old ways weren't broken?'

'I just thought it would be interesting for the viewers.'

'And you thought that without watching it for yourself to be sure it would even make for good viewing.'

'It took so much time to organise that I needed to get it out for the deadline.'

'Yes. It did take more time to organise. It also cost more money to set up too.'

'I'll admit it was a gamble but I thought…'

'You aren't paid to think. You are paid to ensure that everything runs smoothly.'

Nate gave a half-arsed smile as he said, 'It did run smoothly at least.'

'It did?'

'I like to think so.'

'So you have the paperwork in order?'

Nate hesitated. 'I do.'

'For all participants?'

Nate shifted in his seat.

'Want me to answer it for you?' Sharon looked at him with a raised eyebrow. She didn't wait for him to answer. 'No. No you didn't get the paperwork in order for everyone. You got one signature.'

'They agreed…'

'The person who signed up might have but…'

'They said they had talked with…'

'It doesn't matter if they have talked to the whole world, Nate. Without the signature, there is no proof. You put these people on film, in this situation and you did so without the relevant permissions. What happens if we are audited? We can't prove we're running as required by…'

Nate foolishly cut her off and asked, 'What do you want me to do about it? Apologise? I'm sorry. I took a gamble. I got it wrong. I thought the old format was a little stagnant and I tried to breathe a little more life into it. I got it wrong. It won't happen again.' He stopped talking.

For a moment, they both sat in silence.

Sharon slowly smiled. 'No. It won't happen again.' She went quiet again before holding up a DVD. 'Would you like to see it?'

'What's that?'

'What you created. Would you like to see it?'

Nate shrugged. 'Sure.'

Sharon stood up and walked over to the entertainment system along the far wall. She put the DVD into the unit which greedily swallowed it up. She flicked the television on with a press of a button and then made her way back to her desk with the controllers in hand.

She sat down and looked at Nate who was still looking as nervous as he had when he first walked into the room.

'Get you anything?'

Nate looked at her, unsure as to whether she was being serious or not.

'I'm good.'

'Then let us start…'

She raised the controller to the set and hit *play*. The DVD spun to life and the show flickered up on the screen. Sharon sat back in her comfortable leather chair. As Nate watched the screen, her eyes stayed firmly on his face.

PART ONE

HOW MUCH TO

Survive The Night With Your Fears?

Chapter One

Kim Spencer smiled at her husband as he pulled into the driveway of what she liked to call their dream-home. It was a nice property between San Antonio and Austin, Texas. Built some-time in the eighties, it even came with four acres of wooded land.

Kim hadn't long got in from work. She was a licensed vocational nurse working in various homes around the area, something that she had been doing for ten years now. Something that was, better yet, due to stop as she was gearing up to quit work in order to become a full-time student. Even at the age of forty, it was never too late to start again and get chasing those dreams once missed, and this was her chance. Or rather, this was her *second* chance. Kim's plan was to earn an associates degree and become a proper registered nurse and nothing was going to stop her doing that.

The audience, watching at home, were drip-fed this information via titles on the screen. A little background as to why Kim was doing any of this.

'Good day?' She called out to her husband, Jim, as he climbed out of his 69 AMX. He stretched his back and - even from where Kim was standing - she could hear his spine click back into place. Clearly he'd had a heavy day up on the rooves of local buildings, working the sheet metal. To her question, he shrugged.

'Same old.' He double checked the time on his watch. 'You're home late?'

'I had an errand to run,' she said.

Jim shrugged as he approached his wife. He gave her a kiss on the cheek and a little cuddle.

'You stink,' she said.

Jim laughed. 'Been hot as hell and I've had no shade. If you're good, I might just have a shower before I come near you again.'

She laughed. 'I mean, I don't mind it.'

'You're filth!' He stepped around her and made his way to the front door. Kim locked up her car and followed after him.

The screen paused.

*

'Do you see the problem?' Sharon was still looking at Nate who hadn't taken his eyes from the screen in her office. She explained, 'The people watching this… They're already bored. They don't care about the life stories of those they watch. They only want to see…'

She pressed a button on the controller and the television screen flicked to another, seemingly *live*, channel.

On-screen, Angela Mcbride sat back in what looked like a dentist's chair with her mouth open wide. At first sight, anyone coming by this channel would presume she was about to have dental work done but they couldn't be further from the truth.

In the office, Nate asked, 'What is this?'

Sharon answered him, 'Do you honestly think we only have the one channel running?'

The door to the pretend dentist's room opened and a group of teenagers walked in. Made up of both sexes and from all walks of life, they only had one thing in common. They each suffered from terrible acne.

Angela closed her eyes as the first of the teenagers approached where she was sitting. The young lad stopped next to Angela's face and leaned down towards her open mouth, pointing the biggest zit towards her tongue.

'Okay, you can go right ahead,' a voice said from somewhere off screen.

The teenager raised his fingers up to the throbbing zit and squeezed it. The spot only needed the slightest of pressure to explode its white cream out and onto Angela's tongue. Angela flinched but, mercifully, it wasn't as bad as she had imagined.

The lad stepped to the side and a girl took his place. The pus from her spot, when squeezed, snaked out like a worm made of cream. The colour was more yellow than white and the pus needed encouragement from the girl's dainty finger to knock it loose from her skin. She smeared it on Angela's lip where it clung like a crazy glue. Angela knew the rules and licked her lip clean. She gagged but, again, only because she knew what was happening and not because it was *that* bad.

'Okay that's enough,' the voice said. Angela visibly breathed a sigh of relief as she coughed. The voice continued, 'That was just the appetiser. A tease. What we have actually prepared is a little more substantial than that.' The person laughed.

The door opened again and a man in a lab coat walked in. Clutched in his hand was a glass beaker the size of a pint glass. The beaker itself was filled with a fondue of collected cheese squeezed from zits, pimples and spots.

Angela looked at the beaker with fear. She immediately retched as the man stepped to the side of her and ordered her to stick out her tongue.

Without a further word, he reached into the inside pocket of his jacket and pulled out a plastic spatula. With that, he scooped up a healthy dollop of pus before, with a look of glee in his eyes, he smeared it across Angela's tongue like he was putting jam on a slab of bread; a thick layering.

Angela's eyes streamed as she continually retched. Somehow, she managed to keep from adding to the pus with an acidic pool of vomit.

'Now eat it.'

She closed her mouth and scraped the mixture off her tongue using the roof of her mouth. The moment a little bit came away from her tongue, she swallowed it down hard whilst trying to pretend it was something else entirely.

In the office, Sharon said, 'The audience don't know the woman's name. They don't care about it either. All they care about is how much she said she would want to carry out this task and how it will be when she actually *does* carry it out. There's no life story. There's no lessons to be learned. There's nothing on show but the greed, and desperation, of humans.

Sharon flicked the button on the controller again and switched back to the paused introduction of what Nate had been responsible for.

'We collected the pus from hospitals. It cost us nothing but a donation, which we gladly made. You, meanwhile, have had to set cameras up in, and around, this person's home at a cost of...' Sharon leaned towards some paperwork on her desk and shifted through it. She saw the figure she was looking for and her eyes went wide. She exhaled slowly. 'In cameras alone, you have spent more than the entire production of what we are putting that other lady through...'

Sharon raised her eyebrows as Nate refused to say anything. She unpaused the screen.

Chapter Two

'How come?' Jim kicked his shoes off in the hallway, just as he always did, and looked at his wife with a look of confusion on his face. To start with, he thought he had missed an important date, like her birthday or something, but he soon realised it was just another normal day. Which made her announcement that little more surprising.

'I just feel as though we haven't seen them for a while and that it would be nice to have them over,' Kim said. She was talking about her older sister, Linda, and Linda's other-half, Dave. For reasons Jim was still trying to fathom, she had inexplicably decided to invite them over for dinner that evening, despite both Jim and Kim having to work the next day meaning they couldn't even make it a late one. Kim asked, 'It's not a problem, is it?'

Jim hesitated. 'I mean, it would have been nice to know. That's all I'm saying.'

'I'm telling you now.'

'I meant earlier.'

'I'm sorry. I didn't think it would be a problem.' She asked, 'Would you like me to cancel them?'

Jim shook his head. 'I'm sorry. It's been a long day. No, you don't need to cancel them but I will just go and jump in the shower before they get here. As you so rightly pointed out, I fucking stink.' He leaned close to his wife and gave her a peck on the cheek before he made his way up the stairs. Any other day, she might have joined him in the shower for a little fun. A nice way to make him feel a little de-stressed from the day. Not today though. Her eyes darted around the walls and the pictures which hung there. She couldn't see the cameras but she knew they were there.

The screen paused and then fast forwarded. The husband and wife team skipped around from room to room in fast motion as Sharon pushed forward with the tape. Nate watched in silence. She hit unpause again as Kim's sister and her partner entered the building.

'Well this is a nice surprise,' Linda said.

Her husband, Dave, was less enthusiastic. Like Jim, Dave had had a busy day at work and had been looking forward to getting in and watching the game on the television. The last thing he wanted to do was get up off his arse and go and be sociable round someone else's house.

'New coat?' Kim took her sister's coat from her and hung it over the bannister. It wasn't to Kim's taste but she recognised it as being an expensive jacket. Funny really, especially as her sister always moaned at her for being bad with money (and Kim was, to be fair) and yet here she was with the latest fashion, again. Kim didn't say anything though. She knew her sister would have an answer; something along the lines of how she had known that the coat was being released soon and so had budgeted accordingly.

'Nice, isn't it?'

'Just go through to the kitchen,' Kim said.

Linda knew the way and so did as instructed. Dave and Jim followed behind. Kim hesitated a moment and took in a few deep breaths as though trying to steady some well-hidden nerves. She knew something was going to happen and she knew it would be unpleasant. It had to be for the amount of money that had been discussed. She just didn't know *what* was coming. And the reason she had invited her sister around? Strength in numbers.

*

'We're over thirty minutes in now,' Sharon said. 'And what has happened? They're having a dinner party... The viewing figures by this point; people were turning off by their thousands.' She raised the controller back to the television and swapped channels back to what was happening with Angela, the woman who'd previously been forced to eat spot pus. 'Let's compare,' Sharon said.

The viewing figures had all but doubled.

On-screen, Angela was sitting at a table watching another person who was sitting opposite. The other person, Steven Edwards, was a previous contestant. He wasn't playing the game this time though. He had just come back in another capacity to get a little extra money for himself.

A voice instructed him, 'Okay. When you're ready.'

Steven looked at the small plastic tub in front him.

'It's pretty small,' Steven said, with reference to the tub. Angela smiled. There wasn't much else she could do.

'Hopefully only a little bit will go in there then,' she said.

Steven looked at her. It was hard to feel sorry for her. She had played the game. She had answered the question as to how much she would want to complete this task. Her bids were lowest and so, here she was… Now was the time to put her money where her mouth was. She completed the tasks, she won the money. It was that simple.

'Okay then,' Steven said, psyching himself up for what he needed to do. He knew he had the easy job of the two but it still wasn't pleasant.

'I'm not sure I can watch,' Angela said. She turned away and closed her eyes. A moment later and she thought to raise her hands to her ears too. She pushed a finger into each in order to drown out the noise in the room.

Steven took in a deep breath and slowly exhaled it. Then, he raised two fingers to his open mouth and slowly inserted them. He gagged. He always did have a bad gag reflex but, now he needed more than to just gag.

He pushed his fingers deeper into his mouth, pushing them down on his surprisingly dry tongue, feeling the little taste buds in the process. As his fingers pushed closer to the back of his mouth, he gagged again. It was a little more violent this time and he felt a pull in his stomach as it twisted. He hesitated a moment and then pushed on.

This time when he gagged, a little bile rose up from the pit of his stomach. The strong acidic taste and the congealed texture at the back of the throat, hanging heavy there, caused another gagging reflex which, in turn, brought up more stomach shit. Purely on instinct, Steven leaned over the plastic tub where he promptly spewed out the foul tasting mess. The dense liquid was hot in his mouth and with the same consistency of bitty yoghurt; thoughts he wished he didn't have as they caused him to vomit up more.

Angela scrunched her eyes up tighter. Her fingers blocked some of the noises out but not all of them and it was all she could do not to throw up her own mixture into the little plastic tub too. As she was sitting there, she was questioning her life and what had brought her to this stage. How desperate had she been to agree to play this fucking game? She wanted to back out and to run but she knew, as per their terms, there was no option to do that now. She was signed in for the duration. Besides, she had come this far. She just needed to get it finished with. Get it finished with? That didn't happen just by sitting here, waiting for him to stop spewing. There weren't rules for how much she needed to devour here; only that she needed to eat some, with a spoon no less.

She took a finger from her ear and blindly reached for the spoon resting in her lap. She took it up and reached for tub as Steven turned away and continued throwing up onto the tiled floor. Still with her eyes closed, Angela pulled the tub towards her and tilted it to a slight angle to ensure the sick collected up to an easy depth to spoon out. The last thing she wanted to do was to fuck around with trying to spoon it out. Just get it done. That was all that was going around and around in her mind now. Just get it done.

She refused to open her eyes still. Out of sight, out of mind. Angela dipped the spoon into the tub and shovelled it to the corner of the tub, where she'd presumed she had tilted the liquid. When she thought she had a spoonful, she set the tub down and raised the spoon up to her mouth.

The smell.

She retched.

Cabbage, acid, rotten meat, bin juice, all mixed together with the stink of someone's rancid breath when they are found to be suffering from severe halitosis.

Angela retched again but managed to save herself from adding to the already grim concoction.

In the office, Nate felt his own stomach twist and turn on the inside. If there was one thing he personally hated, it was seeing someone throw up. He didn't need to be in the room with Angela to know how it would smell. He certainly didn't need to be seeing what she was going to have to do. He looked away.

Sharon said, 'And yet look at the viewing figures.'

More and more people were tuning in as viewers told their friends what was happening, getting them to tune in too.

On-screen, Angela tipped the spoon into her mouth. The soup (for that's all she told herself it was) was hot in her mouth. Lumpy. Vegetable soup. Nothing more and nothing less. She swallowed and immediately coughed it back up into her mouth as her own body said *fuck that*. She forced it down again by swallowing harder. This time it stayed but her stomach immediately complained with a loud rumble.

Keep it down, she mentally told herself. *Keep it down.*

'More,' the voice told her.

Angela didn't waste any time. She scooped up another spoonful, still refusing to look at it. Again, like eating a nicely prepared soup, she gingerly tipped the spoon's contents into her mouth, via pursed lips so as not to spill any down her chin. Still hot in the mouth. Still disgusting in flavour and, worse, this time she felt something almost stringy in texture land upon her tongue. *Don't think about it.* Regurgitated food? A lump of stomach lining? Quickly, she swallowed.

'I don't need to see any more,' Nate said.

Sharon was unfazed by all of this. She had seen this before and worse. To her, the only thing that troubled her these days was the shit that Nate had produced with his first solo scenario he had developed. *That* was the kind of crap that twisted her insides.

Sharon flicked back to Nate's tape and started to fast forward through it once more. Twelve hours. That's how long it went on for. Twelve fucking hours.

Chapter Three

'How are Austin and Shelby?' Linda asked.

Austin and Shelby were Kim's kids. Austin was 21 years old and Shelby was 19. Shelby was living away, at college, whilst her brother had his own apartment fairly local to Kim.

'Yeah, they're good I think,' Kim said. Whilst she wasn't a bad mother, or even didn't enjoy hearing from her children, Kim liked to give them the space they needed to grow up. She didn't spend every day chasing them up to check they were okay. She knew, as did they, that if they had any problems or concerns with life, all they had to do was pick up a phone and she would be there for them.

'The fucking light has come on again,' Jim said in a little world of his own. As they were all sitting around the table, enjoying a hot pot Kim had made, Jim, facing the window, had noticed a light. Even though the blinds were closed, he could still see through the small crack that the security light outside kept going on and off again, as though someone was out there and pacing.

Kim said, 'It's probably just the cat.' Along with owning a pitbull rescue (Emma), a little shepherd mix rescue (Mickie) and an old blind and deaf bulldog called Lola, Kim and Jim also had an outdoor cat named Bartleby. In Kim's own words, he was an asshole. 'He probably knows you're watching for the light and doing it on purpose. You know what a dick he is.'

Jim had no comment to that. The cat was a little dick. Even so, he couldn't help but think it strange that the light was going on and off so frequently. Whether the cat was an idiot or not, he didn't tend to just pace the house like that and - despite Kim's thoughts - Jim couldn't see the little bastard doing it on purpose just to fuck with him.

Jim set his cutlery down and walked over to the window. He peered out, through the small crack in the blinds.

'I can't see anything,' he said.

'It's just the cat,' Kim told him. Unbeknownst to the others, her heart rate had increased slightly and she was sure her face was starting to flush. Whilst she didn't know what was happening out there, she had a very good suspicion that it was absolutely nothing to do with the cat. She tried to get Jim back to the table. 'Come and eat your food before it gets cold,' she said.

He didn't.

Jim walked over to the back door. First he unlocked it, with a twist of the key they kept in the lock, and then he turned the handle, pulling the door towards him (and open in the process).

The warm air immediately hit as he stepped out onto the back porch.

'Maybe you should go with him?' Linda looked at Dave who, despite watching Jim, hadn't stopped eating his food.

'He's got it under control.'

From out of sight now, Jim called out, 'The fuck is this?'

Kim was almost too afraid to ask, 'What's what?'

'There's a huge lump of cheese out here.'

Kim's face flushed red and, again, her heart skipped a beat.

'You go shopping earlier and drop it? Why the fuck do we need so much cheese? Damn thing is the size of a fucking bowling ball...'

'Just leave it. Come back in.'

'I'm not going to leave it out here...'

Outside, out of sight, Jim approached the block of cheese. As he did so, he stopped at the sound of heavy footsteps running towards him from around the corner of the house. He looked up to see who, or what, it was and ——

There was a strange sound of metal sliding shut first and then a heavy thump from outside as though something large had hit the porch's wooden decking. Kim didn't dare move as she called out, 'Jim?'

Jim didn't answer.

Linda again looked at Dave and ordered him, 'Go and see what is going on out there for God sake!'

'Okay, okay...'

Dave grabbed a napkin from the table and dabbed it over the corners of his mouth, cleaning away any debris food. He tossed it down next to his plate and stood up, as both Linda and Kim stayed firmly rooted to their seats.

'What's going on out...' Dave stopped in the doorway.

The screen paused.

*

'It's already far too long,' Sharon said, looking at the screen. 'It would have been better had we seen what happened to the husband but, you couldn't even get that.'

Nate felt his face burn with embarrassment. They should have had the footage but the exterior camera, covering that particular angle, had failed. All footage lost with only static visible.

'We don't want to see reactions,' Sharon said. 'We want to see action.'

'It was a technical issue,' Nate admitted.

'You spend all that money, setting things up, and you have a technical issue?'

Had there been no *technical issue*, the audience would have been treated to the sight of a six foot *character* running up to Jim and swinging a bear-trap straight at the man's face. The jaws of the device literally ripped through the front half of his face. The metal teeth cleanly cut through and left him staggering on the spot with the cross-section of the inside of his head on display for all to see. From there, he dropped to his knees and then to his side. When he hit the deck, the inside of his head slipped out and splattered onto the cold wooden slats of the porch area as the murderer ran back off into the darkness.

'Look at this,' Sharon said as she changed the channel back to the other film she'd been showing Nate.

Angela pointed to Steven Edwards and said, 'I choose him.'

She didn't want to choose anyone but, that was what she had previously agreed to do. Choose any other person from the group to perform the act upon. At least Steven was already in the room so she could just get it over and done with and move on to whatever was meant to be next.

Steven looked shocked that he had been chosen. He didn't say anything though as Angela positioned herself on the floor in front of him. She reached up and fumbled for his belt buckle. She first opened that and then unbuttoned his jeans. She pulled them down, along with his shorts, to reveal a sorry-looking, flaccid prick. But then, what did she expect? He *had* just been throwing up and then watching her eat his sick… It wasn't exactly a sight to get him in the mood.

Despite the state of his dick, Angela took it between her fingers and put it in her mouth in the hope that the warm, wetness of it would stir the cock to life.

Sharon said, 'One camera. One person in the next room watching the stream. A spare camera ready to go, if there are any issues. This method hasn't failed us yet. The first time you set out, on your own, and change things… You have issues.'

Nate was watching the on-screen action. It wasn't the camera letting the show down this time. It was the gentleman's inability to seemingly get an erection, not that Nate was judging him. He wasn't sure if he'd be able to under those circumstances either; the stink of sick lingering in the air and on both of their breath.

'He isn't getting hard,' Angela said to someone out of sight. Angela looked over in their direction. As she did so, she continued stroking Steven's soft cock. Steven himself was visibly embarrassed.

From behind the scenes, there was a sigh. The voice told her, 'We just want to see someone squirt in your mouth. We never said it had to be with ejaculate.'

'I'm really sorry about this,' Steven said as he looked down to where Angela was kneeling. He retched when he noticed she was kneeling in his puddle; a sight which distracted him from the way she was currently looking at him.

Without a word she put his little prick back in her mouth. Despite not getting hard at it, the sensation was still pleasant and he couldn't help but to let out an audible sigh.

She bobbed her head up and down his shaft once more, in one last ditch attempt to get him hard. When she realised it definitely wasn't to happen, she clamped her jaw shut hard. Steven screamed in agony as her canines pierced the spongy flesh of his penis. Undeterred by his screams, Angela yanked her head back and to the side. At first Steve's cock stretched but then the skin ripped. Like a dog with a toy, Angela started to shake her head from side to side with a startling ferocity. Steven continued to scream.

'Jesus Christ,' Nate said as he crossed his legs.

'Brutal? Yes.' Sharon pointed to the figures at the bottom of the screen. 'Look at them. They're all tuning in. They love it. They *want* this. They don't want what you produced.'

Nate didn't say anything. What was there to say? The viewing figures spoke for themselves. He had already apologised too. What else was there?

Angela pulled away and spat the severed cock from her mouth as Steven fell to the floor with his hands covering the now-bloody leftovers.

The unseen voice said, 'We want to see him spurt. We aren't seeing that.'

Blood was coming from the fresh wound but, true enough, it wasn't spurting out. Had there been an erection in place, with all blood pumping to the hard-on, it could have been a different story but, nope. There definitely wasn't a good enough spurt to get Angela through to the next round.

Still in a frenzy, she grabbed the spoon she'd earlier used for the sick eating. She turned it around so that she held the head in the palm of her hand and - without warning - she jarred the handle directly into Steven's jugular. His scream changed pitch as she pulled the makeshift weapon from his neck only to coated in a heavy spurt of bright red claret.

Angela pushed herself back along the floor until her back was against the wall. There she stayed as she watched Steven thrash around, spraying the last of his blood all around the once-white room.

Angela dropped the spoon to the splattered floor.

The voice congratulated her, 'Well done.'

'Meanwhile,' Sharon said as she switched the screen back to Nate's taping. 'What do we have here?'

Chapter Four

Kim screamed as Dave stopped her from running to see what had happened to her husband. He pulled her back into the house and kicked the door shut with the heel of his foot.

'You don't need to see,' Dave warned her.

'I want to! I need to!'

'No!' Dave kept hold of her, despite the way Kim was squirming in his arms. The dogs were barking at all the commotion and Linda was standing, backed into the corner of the room - scared out of her mind.

'We need to call the police!' Linda scrambled forward for her phone which rested on the table. A quick glance at the screen and - no signal. It was usually full here but, not today. Not with *them* blocking it, not that she knew this. To her, it was just a dead zone which did happen from time to time with her provider. She dropped the phone down and hurried across to where Kim's house-phone was attached to the wall. That too was dead. The outside line having been cut not long after Linda and Dave had arrived at the property. 'It's dead! The phones are dead!'

'He wasn't supposed to be killed!' Kim was screaming over and over. 'He wasn't supposed to be killed!'

Dave just held onto her, ignoring her words and holding her tightly as he struggled to make sense of what was going on. His head... Jim's head had been clean cut in half! How does that even happen?!

'Where's your cell?' Linda turned to Kim in the hope that her own phone was close to hand. Better yet, that it had some service. At least enough to send a text to 911.'

'You realise we don't have any agreements with the United States with regards to our little games, right?'

'It was all cleared.'

'By whom?'

'Me. All the paperwork is in order.'

'And I should take your word for that?'

'I can get it on your desk within the day.' Nate added, 'The idea was to expand. Bring something new to the table and expand. That's what I did.'

'No. That's what you tried to do.'

'Where's your phone?!' Linda shouted, snapping Kim back to reality. Her sister pointed through to the front room.

'Through there. On the coffee table.'

Linda ran through to the living room. True enough, Kim's cell was resting on the coffee table just as she had said. Linda grabbed it and immediately noticed that it too had no service.

'Shit... Shit... *Shit...*'

Movement from the window caught her eye. Linda looked up and screamed at the sight of a giant white mouse staring directly at her through the double-glazed window. The mouse raised its hand and slowly waved at her before it turned and walked from sight.

'What is it?' Dave called from the other room as Linda walked over to the window and peered out, craning her head to try and see where the mouse had gone.

She saw nothing.

'Linda? What is it?'

'There's someone outside.'

It was a someone and not a some*thing*. She knew it wasn't an actual mouse but, instead, an idiot dressed as one for some reason.

Dave entered the room with a clearly traumatised Kim by his side. 'What did you see?'

Linda slowly turned to face him. *How was she to explain what the fuck she saw?* 'I saw…' She hesitated a moment before she just blurted it out. 'There was a person dressed up as a mouse out there.'

'A fucking mouse?'

'Just a white costume with red eyes… A mouse!' She immediately turned to Kim and asked, 'What have you dragged us into?'

Linda didn't know that any of this was Kim's fault. All she knew was that Kim had invited them around for the evening and now bad things were happening. Had they not been invited, Linda and Dave would still be at home. Dave would be watching the game and Linda would be doing anything but *this*. So, whilst she didn't realise that all of this actually was Kim's fault, what she did know was that they wouldn't be standing there now if not for her invite.

Kim didn't have a chance to answer as Linda said, 'Her phone has no service either. We're going to have to make a run for the car.' The moment she finished speaking, Linda started towards the door. Kim reached out and grabbed her sleeve, pulling her back.

Kim immediately panicked. 'We can't go out there.'

'There is someone *out* there! We can't stay in here!'

Linda looked to her husband for support. He had made his way over to the window and was squinting out of it, trying to see if anyone was still out there or whether they could make a run for the car.

'Can you see them?' Linda took a step forward.

Dave squinted harder.

When he didn't immediately answer, Linda raised her voice. 'Dave. Can you see anything?'

'I can see...'

The glass smashed first and, before the fragments even had a chance to fall to the floor, Dave's head jolted backwards as though violently hit by something unseen. Linda and Kim screamed as Dave then fell, backwards, to the floor. There, they could clearly see the hole in his head, right between his open eyes. His blood immediately started to soak into the carpet beneath his body.

Linda ran over to Dave's body. She crouched down next to him and pulled him up off the floor, cradling his corpse close to her chest with tears streaming down her face.

'Get away from the window,' Kim said as the dogs continued to bark at the top of their lungs. 'Shut up! Please! Just shut up!'

This time, Kim heard the gun shot as it rattled through the air. With the window already smashed, the bullet passed straight through, directly into Linda's head. She dropped dead on the spot, right next to her husband as Kim screamed again.

The screen paused.

'See another difference between what you are doing here, or rather what you *did* here, and what we do with the main shows?' Sharon looked at Nate, expecting some kind of answer from him.

'I'm not sure what you mean.'

'We've had some much time getting to know them, hearing about them and - straight away - you've killed three of the four people.'

'We have.'

'All that time getting to know them and look at how fast you have killed them. With the exception of the first man, killed in a bear-trap, it's not even showing imagination either. *And* you fucked the first one up by not actually showing it the way our audience would have wanted. So, the one good kill you did have, you missed. The other kills... Really? A bullet?'

'It was never about the others... It was only ever about the one woman.'

Sharon flicked the television station back to Angela. Angela was banging on a mirror. She was aware that, behind it, there were people watching her movements.

'Let me out!' She was screaming over and over again. Around her mouth, Steven's blood was smeared where she'd bitten off his penis. Steven's body was in the background of the shot; a pained expression etched upon his face. 'I don't want to play anymore! I want to go home!'

Sharon spoke over the television as it continued to play in the background, 'It's not about the other people. It's only ever about the *one* person who won the game, is it not? In this case, it is a woman called Angela Mcbride. She won the game, she has to play it through. Those are the rules. But look at that…' Sharon pointed to the body at the back of the shot. 'It's not about him but if we have room to make more people suffer for the entertainment of others, we take it. So your shitty little film wasn't about the other people in the house? So what? Killing them as fast, as you did, is nothing more than a waste. I take it, like in this country, we have to pay for the dead? With that in mind, we make sure it is cost effective. We capitalise on their deaths in whatever way we can. But, no, you come along and put a bullet in them and just move on as though they were nothing.

People see people get shot all the time. You've given them nothing new. Nothing to talk about. Nothing to be horrified about. It's just dull.' She pointed back to the screen again and said, 'Unlike this.'

Angela was sitting back at the sick-splattered table again. In her hand she had a small pair of tweezers. The idea of the next *game* was simple; she simply had to remove her finger-nails.

At first Angela tried to ease them out. She gripped the nail hard and tight and gently rocked up and down with the tweezers. She could feel the nail moving but not in the way it needed to. The skin was moving with the nail thanks to its elasticity; it didn't mean the nail was going to come out. For that, she quickly realised, that all she could do was to literally rip up and back, towards her body, with the tweezers.

Angela closed her eyes. She took a couple of deep breaths and…

'Did you watch what we did?' Nate looked away from the screen and straight at Sharon who, herself, was engrossed in what Angela was doing. Sharon slowly looked over to him. He asked again, 'Did you watch the whole tape?'

'I'll be honest, no. This is the point in which I turned it off because it is quite clear you have no idea how to put on a good show.'

'Then you missed the best bit.'

'I doubt that.'

'I said, the show wasn't about the people she had in the house. It was only about her and how much money would she want to survive a night based on her worst fears.' He explained, 'One of her worst fears is to be alone. To make that happen we had to quickly kill off the other people. The whole time she had company, she wouldn't be living her fear. Now look though, she's in her house and she is alone, with the exception of their dead bodies. She knows we are coming for her. She knows what she has signed up for. She knows that we have no issues murdering people. She is petrified.'

'So now we have people tuning in to watch a woman piss in her pants?'

'No. Now you have a woman who is about to meet her worst fears in the worst way she can possibly imagine.'

Sharon sighed. She cleared her throat and impatiently asked, 'So what are her worst fears?'

Nate smiled. 'I think you'll be happy. Press play.'

Chapter Five

'You can fast forward this bit,' Nate said.

*

The show played through in fast motion as Kim ran around the house in a blind state of panic, securing the windows and doors as best as she could. She also stopped by the phones a few times in order to check them for any sign of signal but - the lines to the house were cut and cellular service remained blocked.

By the time the fast-forward stopped, Kim was huddled over on the hallway floor. She clutched a kitchen knife close to her chest as she openly wept both because of the deaths and because of the fear surging through her body.

There was a loud knock at the door; three successive bangs, one after the other with only the slightest of beats between the hits. Each one made her visibly jump.

In order to be able to defend herself better, Kim stood up, pointing the knife towards the front door. She was unaware that another series of knocks was about to come from the rear of the house.

KNOCK! KNOCK! KNOCK!

Kim jumped again and spun on the spot so that she was facing the back of the house. She knew there was no way it was the same person who'd knocked on the front door. No way did they have time to get around to the back of the house to knock again.

'Leave me alone!' She screamed, 'I don't want to do this anymore! I've changed my mind!'

In the office, Sharon laughed. So many people say the same thing; *they don't want to play anymore. They've changed their minds. They want to go home. They've made a mistake… Blah blah fucking blah.*

Kim screamed as the front door was suddenly kicked in. Standing there, a gun clutched in its hand, was a large mouse of just over six foot in height.

A similar sound came from the back of the house as the back door was kicked in.

Kim screamed, 'Leave me alone! I've changed my mind!'

All three dogs ran towards the intruder, barking. Without a warning and without a word, the mouse simply raised its weapon and fired three deadly shots. The animals crashed to the floor, instantly stopped in their tracks by the sudden lump of lead. Kim screamed again as she raised her knife in readiness to defend herself, not that such a weapon was a match against a bullet.

The mouse stepped in. Another stepped in behind it who was also carrying a weapon.

With tears streaming down her petrified face, Kim asked, 'Why are you doing this?' But she knew *why*. She had signed up to this. She had welcomed it to her home by putting her own signature upon the presented contract. Had she not signed, she would be enjoying a quiet evening with Jim. Had she not signed, they'd all still be breathing.

Kim turned to face the other group as they stepped into the hallway behind her. Another two mice. One had a gun and the other had a syringe. She twisted her whole body and pointed the knife at them.

'Stay back!'

The group from the front of the house took another step forward closer and she turned back to them, unsure as to who was the bigger threat of the two groups. Then, they both stopped moving. Instead, they were just standing there silently.

Kim yelled, 'What do you want?!'

'Squeak.' The first of the mice, from the front of the house, said it again, 'Squeak.' He wasn't mimicking the sound of rodent. He was just saying the word. 'Squeak. Squeak...' Over and over again as the other *mice* started to do the same until they were all doing it in unison.

Kim screamed.

*

Sharon looked at Nate in disbelief. 'Is this a joke?'

'What do you mean?'

'You have people dressed up as mice and it's supposed to entertain an audience who is expecting...' She raised the controller up and flicked the channel back to what was happening in the other session.

Angela was on the tiled floor. Her eyes were staring up to the ceiling, unblinking. Her throat cut wide open with but a small bubble of blood coming from it. The floor, and walls, were sprayed in the rest of her body's blood. A man was standing over her corpse with a knife in his hand.

The unseen voice explained, 'As the second highest, you get to pick up from where the previous contestant left off, after she refused to do more of the tasks. By taking her life, you have already made it so you don't need to revisit the tasks she has completed. Please introduce yourself to the viewers.'

The man looked directly to the camera. 'My name is Christopher Burrell.'

'And you agree that you have played the game, along with the other contestants, and came out second with the amount bid?'

'I do.'

'And you know what comes next?'

'I do.'

'Then let the games continue.'

The door opened and a man walked in. The stranger led a pig in via a lead around the animal's neck. He stopped close to the table and tied the pig's lead to the leg of the bolted down bit of furniture. The man looked at Christopher and nodded. He said, 'Good luck.'

Christopher didn't thank the stranger as he promptly left the room. Instead, he looked towards the animal before taking a few steps towards it. The pig reacted nervously, unsure as to the man's intentions.

'It's okay,' Christopher said. 'It's all good,' he spoke in a soothing voice. The pig wobbled a little on its feet but, other than that, made no more attempts to move away as Christopher slowly knelt down alongside it. He put one arm around the beast and gently pulled it close to him. He moved his other hand to the rear of the animal and lined his index finger up with the beast's anus.

Christopher closed his eyes as, with a strong arm, he pushed his finger up inside the pig. This wasn't a sexual thing. He wasn't supposed to be getting off, or getting the pig to climax. This was all about the taste.

The pig screeched and struggled as Christopher struggled to hold it steady. He circled his finger around and around inside the pig before pulling it back out. The withdrawal was accompanied by the sound of a wet, squelchy "pop" noise. No sooner had he released the pig did he back away to the other side of the room, just in case it tried to turn and bite him for violating it.

What he had just done - that wasn't the *game*. That was merely part of it. His game was… Christopher didn't look at the state of his finger. Had he done so, he would have seen it tinted a light brown in colour. He just opened his mouth and inserted his finger. Once inside, he clamped his mouth shut and, with his tongue pressed against his digit, he slowly pulled it back out. In the process of withdrawing; his tongue licked the finger spotlessly clean.

Still with his eyes closed tight, he swallowed hard.

'It kind of tastes like gone off bacon,' he said.

Sharon turned to Nate and asked him, 'Having watched that, do you honestly believe our audience would be happy with people dressed up as giant mice? You really think the kind of people who like this,' she pointed to the screen, 'are going to be entertained by...' She flicked back to Nate's tape. The screen was still paused on the sight of the white mouse-dressed intruders.

'She's scared of mice.'

'And that might well be true but it doesn't exactly make for good television now, does it?'

'This is just setting the scene.'

'You've been setting the scene for long enough and you've seen the viewing figures and what the audience thinks of that particular tactic...'

'I know that now. I didn't at the time.'

'We have a winning formula.'

'I thought I could do it better.'

'And you have shown yourself up in the process and made us question your value within our business.'

'So I'm getting sacked?'

'You've had a woman chased around her own house by people dressed up in fancy-dress. Did you honestly think you would keep your job?'

'I tried something new!'

'As you keep saying and yet nothing is fixed.'

'I learned some lessons.'

'Which cost us viewers and money. What if those viewers don't come back? What if it was their first time on to our sites? What if they logged on, hated what they saw and decided it's not for them? They log off, they find some other form of entertainment instead. We lose money. Worse yet; they tell their friends about the show and their friends don't bother to check it out for themselves. You've heard about people who receive bad customer service?'

'What do you mean?'

'Statistics show people are more likely to talk about bad customer service they've received over the good that they might have experienced. People like to complain. They get treated badly, they tell everyone. They have a miserable time, they broadcast it on social media. Poor holiday? Poor reviews. Friends told. They watch a shit television show, they warn their friends… Had it not been for the fact we run multiple shows, you could have ruined us with this crap.'

'It was one poor show. I don't think it would have ruined…'

'You're not paid to think. You're paid to put on a good show for our audience. You failed. And you are certainly not clued up on what makes for a good show so you're not really in a position to state whether something could or could not ruin us. The bottom line is, *you don't know.*'

Nate smiled.

'Something funny?'

'Just that, I might have fucked up on the execution but I *know* you'll love the ending.'

Chapter Six

Kim's dreams were cruel. Her husband, Jim, was sitting opposite her with a look of sheer disappointment on his face. They'd had their arguments over the years, just like any other normal couple, but she'd never seen this expression before. She hadn't wanted to see it either.

His skin was ghostly pale and there was a mistiness over his eyes giving them an almost grey colour. He hadn't said anything to her. He hadn't blamed her for what had happened, even though they both knew it was her fault. He just simply sat there, staring at her with the pair of them surrounded by blackness and nothing.

Kim said to him, 'I'm sorry.'

He either didn't hear her words, or he didn't care to acknowledge them and accept her apology. He certainly made no signs of being even remotely close to forgiving her.

A single tear rolled down her cheek. Usually he hated to see her cry, not that it happened often. On the rare times it had, he had comforted her and reassured her that everything was going to be okay. Not today though. There was a distinct lack of empathy in the way he looked *through* her.

On the off-chance he hadn't heard her, she repeated herself and said, 'I'm sorry.'

Still, nothing. No less than she deserved. She wiped away her tear.

He said to her, 'Wake up.'

'What?'

Jim suddenly jumped to his feet and screamed in Kim's face, 'WAKE UP!'

Kim slowly opened her eyes. Her head was pounding in such a way that she knew she was awake now and no longer dreaming. Her surroundings were similar though; a heavy blackness which she couldn't visually penetrate in order to make anything else out within the room.

'I was just dreaming of this room,' she said to no one. 'Were you in my dreams? Did you make this room to look like the one in my dream?' No one answered. 'My husband was with me. Is he here now?'

The lights flickered on. Her husband wasn't in the room and nor was it a room of her home. She didn't recognise where she was.

'In my dream, he was just sitting opposite me. He wasn't saying anything. He was just staring.' She added, 'He didn't look like my husband though. He just looked like an empty shell...'

Her entire demeanour had changed from the way she'd been acting before she had been injected with the needles. She was calmer somehow. Perhaps due to the residue drugs within her system?

The room was more akin to the ones in which the usual "sessions" took place. Instead of a table bolted to the floor though, there was a bed onto which Kim was strapped. She pulled at her restraints. It was clear she wasn't going anywhere soon. Not unless they let her out at least.

Referring to the restraints, she called out, 'This wasn't one of my fears. You've messed up.' She swallowed hard as she remembered the dead bodies the night had already brought her. The ones *she* was responsible for.

'So what happens next then?' She wanted to call out and demand for them to release her but she knew it wouldn't help. If anything, shouting would only make it worse. If she played it cool, they might come in and move things forward. After all, half of what this was about was the reaction. If she showed no reaction, they wouldn't be getting what they wanted. If only she could turn the clock back and react differently back at the house, she thought. A stupid thought really given that, if she could, she wouldn't just rewind back to the house. She would rewind back to when she first met Nate and heard his offer. She'd go right back to that moment and tell him to stick his offer up his arse.

But she couldn't do that.

There was no rewinding time.

All she could do now was play them at their own game and show them no fear. That was what tonight was about after all - her worse fears. Or rather, surviving a night of her worst fears. She didn't know the time. She had no idea how long she had been out cold for but, morning must be coming. She just needed to see the sun rise and do so with a brave face.

Anyway - there was nothing else they could do to her. They'd killed the people she had loved, they'd killed her pets. They'd shown themselves dressed as mice. What else was there?

The door opened and four white mice walked in, standing tall. Men in fancy dress. They surrounded the bed on which Kim was restrained. One either side, one at the head and one at the foot. They didn't have anything with them. It was just them, standing there, in their costumes.

'So what's next?' Kim looked at each of them in turn, waiting to see who would be the first to speak. No one did. 'You're just going to stand there until morning are you?'

Still, they didn't move.

The screen fast-forwarded.

'I really don't understand how you thought this would be suitable,' Sharon said.

One of the dressed men walked from the room. He returned, pushing a trolley in front of him. On the trolley there were a number of syringes, pre-loaded with something unknown to those watching. There was also a scalpel. Beneath the top layer, there was a second shelf on the trolley. On that there was a box-shaped item, hidden beneath a white cloth.

The *mouse* stopped the trolley next to his colleague. In turn, his colleague took hold of the scalpel. Silently he cut away Kim's top revealing her bare skin and bra beneath.

'Oh? What's this?' Sharon stopped fast-forwarding the action on-screen.

'What are you going to do?' Kim asked. She was trying her best to stay calm but her voice betrayed her with its obvious quiver.

The mouse put the sharp blade against Kim's stomach and went to put pressure on, in order to cut her open. Kim immediately tensed up and closed her eyes as she braced herself for the bolt of pain that was to shoot through her body. There was no pain. There was no cutting.

Kim opened her eyes. The mouse was still holding the scalpel close to her but, instead of just slicing her with it, he reached for the first of the needles. He took it up and jabbed it in her stomach before plunging the liquid into her. Kim winced and let out a little squeal of pain as the coolness of the drug started to travel through her blood system.

'What is it? What *is* it?'

She needn't have worried. This was merely something to numb the area so that the cut wouldn't hurt. This wasn't done for her benefit though; they didn't want her passing out before the fun could really begin.

'Tell me that's not anaesthetic,' Sharon said.

'A necessity.'

'Our audience like the screaming.'

'They might but there's only so much a person can take before they pass out.'

'And then you bring them round again.'

'Or - give them something to help with the pain so they can stay awake for the duration of what we do to them.'

'Without them feeling?'

'Sometimes the mind is worse than the actual pain felt.'

Sharon didn't argue with Nate. On *that* they agreed. The problem was, she hadn't seen much proof that Nate had it in him to come up with something truly horrific… Something that could come even close to being worse than the pain a person could feel.

The mouse set the needle down and then went to dig the scalpel into her skin again. For a second time Kim braced herself only for the mouse to do a mock laugh when he pulled the blade away again. He set it down on the trolley, next to the needles and then nodded to the other mice.

The other mice took his cue and pulled her leggings and panties down and off so that her bottom half was entirely naked. Kim tried to cross her legs to save some dignity but was stopped by the tightness of the restraints. Her bare legs, her pussy and slightly unkept pubic hair were on display for all to see.

'Well at least we have some nudity,' Sharon said. 'Nice to see old-school too. So many people these days prefer the bald look thinking it's what everyone is looking for these days. I don't know. To me it's a little kid-like...'

'Can't say I've given it much thought in that direction. I just think it's tidier and...' Nate stopped talking when Sharon cast him a glance. The look on her face suggested she wasn't up for discussing the art of pubic hair.

The mouse next to the trolley reached down. From under the white sheet, he pulled out a tube of lubricant. He showed Kim before he pushed it between her legs. She winced as the end of the tube was pushed into her ill-prepared pussy. With the tip in, the mouse squeezed hard as he emptied the contents up inside of her.

Kim gasped as she felt the cold wetness fill her. Her heart raced as she could only imagine what they were playing at. Her stomach was now completely numb.

The screen paused.

'I trust we're not just about to get a rape show?'

'We're not.' Nate corrected himself. 'At least not the way you might be thinking.'

'Because rape is not entertaining. It's just desperate men showing their pathetic lack of ability to form a normal relationship and win a woman over with charm.'

Nate didn't highlight the fact that, in the last filming he had been a part of, they'd had a homeless man rape an unconscious woman. He figured that she would just argue how it was never about the rape itself. That was merely a means to an end; to lead to the next *How Much To* that the contestant had to work through. 'And the last thing we need to see is a bunch of men, in fancy dress, rape a bound woman.'

Not for the first time, Nate shifted uncomfortably in his seat. There wasn't going to be any men in fancy dress raping this woman but he knew - at this stage - he was pretty much going to *always* be in the wrong. Whatever holes she could pick in this, she would.

'You just need to keep watching,' Nate said.

Chapter Seven

The screen unpaused. The action continued.

The mouse closest to the trolley reached down and pulled the sheet away from whatever it was covering. There, hidden beneath, was a glass tank with a number of mice scurrying around inside.

The tank was lifted and set down on the top of the trolley within easier reach.

'What are you doing?' Kim started to struggle against the restraints, not that they were going anywhere. The panic was both immediate and obvious. Her number one fear, alongside being left alone? Mice. Not the fancy-dress kind; the *real* kind.

The dressed-up man removed his white glove (part of his shitty costume) and the lid of the tank. He reached in and grabbed the slowest of the rodents, despite its attempt to run away from his hand. Panicked; it squeaked.

'What are you doing?!' Kim was just repeating herself as she watched on with eyes wide in fear.

With the wriggling rodent clasped tightly in his hand, the stranger moved closer to where Kim lay. The face behind the mask slowly turned to look at the petrified woman. She could swear she could sense his smug, sadistic smile beneath.

'Whatever you're thinking… Please don't do it.'

Her words fell upon deaf ears. The masked man put the rodent up against Kim's pussy and - *he pushed.*

Kim screamed as she felt the rodent slip inside her; a process made easier with the force in which it was pushed and the copious amounts of lubricant inside her. She could feel it inside her, wriggling to get out. She could feel its tiny little feet, scratching her as it frantically clawed - trying to burrow for freedom. She screamed again as she could feel the scared animal's teeth as it started to try and gnaw its way back out. Scraping, biting, scratching, wriggling, stretching…

'Get it out! Please! Get it out!'

Another of the men walked over to the tank. He too removed a glove before reaching in and grabbing one of the rodents. It too tried to scurry away from his hand, not that there was anywhere to go.

The other stranger watched on from where he stood with his hand pressed against Kim's vagina, preventing the first of the rodents from backing up out of her. Only when his colleague was close enough did they quickly swap positions. The second mouse was forced inside Kim as she continued screaming.

Sharon slowly turned to Nate. Even she was surprised with the direction this one was taking. Nate was just watching on, smiling as blood started to trickle from the on-screen subject's ruined cunt.

'Those mice aren't small,' Sharon said.

'They're slightly bigger than average.'

On the screen, a third was pushed inside the woman as she continued screaming and squirming around. The third was half a rodent too much and its back end was left hanging from her. Its tail looked like a fucked-up tampon string with the way it thrashed around, hanging from her snatch.

'How many more?'

Nate admitted, 'As you can see, they've found their limit already.'

'Had you started with this, you could have been onto a winner but... Two and a half mice? Too little, too late.'

Nate smiled. He knew what was to come.

The last of the strangers took his mouse over to where Kim lay as his colleague fetched the scalpel from the trolley. He took a step back to allow his friend to get to Kim's numb stomach and, with a smile beneath his mask, he watched as the sharp, sharp blade sliced Kim's stomach open; deep enough to get through the muscle and flesh... Wide enough for the mouse-holding guy to ram his rodent down inside her and push it between her organs.

Kim's screams were almost constant now as she continued wriggling about as much as her restraints permitted. Her words, *Get it out... Please get it out*, just going over and over and over, all falling upon deaf ears.

Another rodent was picked up from the tank. This one was pushed in her mouth. The mouse immediately turned itself around to jump back out, but was stopped with a gloved hand clamped across Kim's mouth. Beneath the costumed-man's heavy hand, Kim gagged as she felt the rodent's tail thrashing around at the back of her throat. Unseen by the viewers at home, Kim's mind had gone back to the conversation she'd had with Nate, ahead of signing on the dotted line of his presented contract.

'So all I have to do, to get the money, is survive a night filled with my fears?'

Nate had given her a reassuring nod before he said, 'Yes. That's it. You survive a night based on your fears and you get the money... If you can't handle it, you get nothing.'

The whole thing had been a trick. There was no surviving this night. Kim's vision blurred as she slipped into a state of unconsciousness.

Sharon turned the tape off and set the television controller down on the table dividing her and Nate. She sighed.

'Let's not beat around the bush,' she said, 'you fucked up.'

'You're not impressed with the last...'

'Let me stop you right there. The end was *okay*. You had some nice ideas but, really, other than stuffing mice inside her - what else is there? It might have been her fear, and she might have been scared but - what else was there for the viewers?'

'Well...'

'Rhetorical question. There's nothing of interest to the rest of the viewers. We already know that. Do you know how?'

'How?'

'The viewing figures.'

Nate felt his armpits tingle as he started to sweat. There was no denying what she was saying. The figures spoke for themselves and, well, they were definitely lacking. Certainly compared to the other shows.

'You know I should sack you?'

'I know I made a mistake. I tried something new. It didn't work. I can go back to the old routine though. I can make something similar and I can get the viewing figures back. You just need to give me a chance…'

'One of your colleagues has already had an idea on how we move forward, as a company, to entice more viewers and, more importantly, keep them there.'

'Can I ask what that is?'

'No. You may not.' Sharon sat back in her seat. 'The question is: How much do you want your job?'

'I need this job. I have a mortgage, a baby on the way… I have…'

'So then… You need to prove it to me.'

'Prove it?'

'How much you want your job. You need to prove exactly how much you *do* want your job…'

Nate shifted in his chair. He felt uneasy as to where this was going.

Sharon continued, 'You're going to play the game with a room full of strangers. If you really want your job, you'll win that round. Then, once you have done that you will complete the actual tasks in the new version of the game that we're testing…'

'You want me to do what we force these people to do?'

'We don't force anyone. If they want to leave in the first stage, they can. They just don't win the money. If you want to leave, you can. You just won't keep your job.' Sharon smiled. 'Tell you what, I'll even throw in the money if you win too. So you get your job and you get the money. Can't be much fairer than that. Or, you can leave now. It's up to you but you need to decide now. There's no going away and thinking this through...' She paused a moment and then asked, 'So what's it to be?'

PART TWO

HOW MUCH TO

Keep Your Job?

Chapter Eight

Nate sat in a small room with other "contestants" all hoping to win a vast amount of money. Except he wasn't playing for the money. He was primarily playing for his job. If Sharon did go ahead and give him the money as well; that would be a bonus. At this stage though, he didn't trust anyone working in these offices and he hadn't for a while, not since the first game when he had walked away with the day's events playing on his jaded mind.

He looked around the room. The other people there were buzzing at the prospect of walking away with a life-changing sum of money in their bank. None of them yet knew what they were really letting themselves in for. Nate didn't warn them. It wasn't his place to. That was a job for whoever was running this particular session.

The door opened and a dark haired woman with a stern expression walked in. Nate instantly recognised her from a previous run-in, in the office staff-room. Her name was Erica Conner. She immediately clocked Nate. For a split second she looked puzzled but the look soon dissipated, only to be replaced with a smile. Nate knew it wasn't a smile of *kindness*.

He looked over to the door she'd entered through. There was a small part of him which was tempted to just get up and leave. Fuck the job, fuck the money. There'd be other work out there. Worst case scenario, he could go get work in a fast food restaurant. It was better than nothing.

But was it?

Nate knew he was on good money here. Certainly a better wage than the average job out there. Hardly surprising given what they were making their staff do though. *You're going to put people through hell but, for that, you get a nice fat pay check.* He sighed. It would be foolish to leave at this stage. He should at least wait and hear what was being lined up for him and the others. If it was really bad, *then* he could leave.

A little voice popped up in his head, *Can you leave though? Really?*

He tried to ignore it but to no avail.

A baby on the way. Debt to pay off. Already in rent-arrears... Can you really leave? You think your better half will be impressed with your inability to hold down a job? Really?

Erica looked around the room. Each of the contestants, with the exception of Nate, had a little card in front of them which had their name printed onto it. Erica glanced at each in turn.

Tracy Teasdale.

Miranda Ehler.

Mae Rawling.

Carol Trainor.

Their ages were mixed - anything from mid-twenties through to early fifties. The lack of male competition was a surprise to Nate though. Usually the sessions were more mixed. Still, it was better for Nate. Men tended to *bid* lower than the ladies for the majority of the things. With less men here, he had less competition in *that* way. The guys bid lower, the girls bid smarter. He still had to think clever if he was to win. At least… If he was to win without just putting *zero* down for everything.

He sat there and listened as Erica went through the rules he had previously helped to give. *There will be ten questions and you have to put down an amount as to how much money you would want to complete such a task. By the end of the ten questions, whoever has bid the lowest amount in* <u>*total*</u> *is the one who* <u>*has*</u> *to go through to complete the tasks. At any stage, contestants are welcome to put their pen down and leave the room. If they do, they will not be permitted to return. They will be out.*

Erica finished explained the rules and glanced from person to person. They are all seemingly paying attention. None of them looked confused. It was a promising start for them to be able to race through these and just get to the juicy parts.

'Okay,' Erica said. 'Is everyone ready?'

No one said that they weren't. Erica took that as her sign to continue. Nate shifted in his seat, making himself as comfortable as he could. He was dreading to hear what Erica - and her team - had come up with.

'Question one…'

Nate braced himself.

'How much to eat a block of lard?'

Tracy looked up from the sheet she'd been looking at; the one onto which she was ready to pen her answers. 'What?'

'How much to eat a block of lard?'

'A block of lard? Like, right from the fridge?' Tracy looked at the others in the room. Some were already writing a figure down. 'Well how big is the block of lard?'

Erica repeated the question, 'How much to eat a block of lard?'

Nate put a dash down on the paper. He knew this was just to ease people into answering the questions. It was disgusting but it wasn't *too* disgusting. There would be much worse to come and those would be the things he'd charge a little more money for.

Tracy continued, 'This is stupid. I mean, surely we need more details in order to make an informed decision?'

Erica just shrugged her shoulders at the woman. There would be no further details given. If she didn't like it, she knew where the door was.

Tracy shook her head in disbelief. Despite wanting more information, she scribbled a number down regardless whilst trying to picture herself carrying through with such a task. *How big was the block? Was there anything to wash it down with? Was there anything to pick it out from between the teeth at least?*

Erica asked, 'Does everyone have a number written down?' She looked straight at Nate who just smiled at her. Like her earlier smile, when she had seen him sitting there, it wasn't a friendly gesture. It was a challenge. *What have you got for me, bitch?* 'So, ready for the second question then?'

Erica pointed a small remote, pulled from her pocket, to a projector which hung from the ceiling. With a click of a button she displayed a picture up on the wall behind her. It was a photograph of a previous contestant whom Nate recognised immediately. Audra Walgenbach.

'This is a lady called Audra Walgenbach. She was a contestant, much like you. She did not win the chance to go for the money but she did walk away with *some* money thanks to helping us out with...' Erica stopped talking. 'Question two: How much to suck on Audra's used tampon.'

'What?!' Tracy couldn't bite her tongue.

'That's disgusting,' Miranda Ehler said as she shook her head.

Nate didn't give a shit. It wasn't his idea of fun but, to some people, this was a fetish. Also, he had some insider information on this one. Audra had been in the first show he put on, with the help of the previous show-runner. That was over a month ago now so the tampon… It wouldn't be fresh. Not fresh? Not dripping in runny blood or stuck with clots. For all he knew, there'd be no flavour to it. His answer mirrored the first he put down as he put another dash through the box.

'I'm not doing it,' Carol said.

'That's fine. You're welcome to leave,' Erica said.

Carol sarcastically said, 'Can I take a shit somewhere first and sell it to you? Maybe you want to use that later?!'

Erica smiled at her and replied, 'I think we're good thank you.'

'Well I wouldn't put it past you.'

'Like I said,' Erica continued, 'you are welcome to leave. Or maybe you just want to put a higher value down to do this?'

'What else did this Audra have to do?'

'We are not at liberty to discuss other contestants and what they may or may not have signed in for. We do have a lot to go through though so, if you're not going to leave, perhaps you would like to put a number down and we can continue?'

Carol huffed yet still scribbled a number down on her sheet. Desperate people do desperate things.

Whilst dropping his own numbers, or lack of numbers so far, Nate couldn't help but think that - so far - this was pretty tame compared to what he'd seen people from Audra's group do. Sure, sucking on a tampon might not be the most pleasant of things to do but it wasn't the worst either. Nate knew from experience. It wasn't the worst by a *long* shot. He glanced up to Erica who was looking around the room, waiting for people to finish thinking their options through. She was impossible to read. Was there worse to come or was he in for an easy ride?

'Question three... Things are going to be a little harder from here on in so, put down how much money you would need to complete such a task because if you stay until the end and you *win*, you will be expected to complete everything. There is no backing out once you get to that stage. Understand?'

Erica looked around the room, waiting to see the responses from people. They were all looking at her. Some looked more nervous than the others and, they had every reason to be.

Erica continued, 'How much to repeatedly drag your teeth along a slab of concrete? Now for this, you will be given a large piece of concrete paving slab. You will be expected to put it in your mouth as though it was a harmonica. You will bite your teeth down upon it so both rows are clamped upon it. Then, you need to rub it back and forth...'

The room was suitably stunned. Mae started to cry but not because she was being made to do it. Before she had come into the room she had been promised the chance of winning money. Money, they said, which could potentially change her life. A woman living with debt, she had already planned what she would do with the money and now, sitting in the room listening to this shit, it was evident she had little to no chance of getting anything.

'I can't do that,' she said.

'What if I were to offer you five million in cash right now?' Nate turned his attention to her. She looked at him with tears streaming down her cheeks. 'If I gave you the cash right here, right now... Are you really saying you would turn it down? Think about it. Would it hurt to do that to your teeth? Yes. Of course. But you would be able to afford the best dentistry to put it right and, while you get fixed, the best medication to take away the pain...'

Erica interrupted, 'You don't have to do anything you don't want to. If you don't believe you can do it, you're free to leave the room. If you want to think about it for a little longer... So long as you leave before the last question... You won't be in with a chance to win the money. Wait until the end and - well... Then it is strictly down to the numbers. If you're the lowest, you have to...'

Frustrated, Miranda blurted out with, 'Can we just get on with this please?' Erica slowly turned and looked at her with a stone-cold expression frozen on her face as she fixed her eyes on the woman who dared interrupt.

Mae continued weeping as she said, 'I just don't think I could do this, even if I were to win… You're basically asking me to grind my teeth down?!' She looked around at the other contestants and asked, 'Do you not know how much it will hurt? How you would look whilst you waited for the mess to heal enough in order to get them fixed properly?'

Erica walked over to the door and opened it. She stood there a moment, watching Mae expectantly. Despite Mae's outburst, she didn't move. Erica shrugged and closed the door before she walked back to the front of the "class".

'Let us continue…'

Chapter Nine

Nate felt sick to his stomach as it bubbled away with stress. When stressed, some people got headaches but not Nate. He was one of those people who got hit by stress straight in the stomach. First, he would feel sick and then he would need to shit. He tried to ignore the bubbling sensation in his gut as that little voice nagged away in his head: *You can't walk out. She'll never forgive you if you lose this job too. You want to lose her? Because you will. You're a failure. And even if she doesn't leave... You think they'll let you stay in the house when you already owe so much money? You'll lose it all. You'll lose it all or you can go home as a winner.*

Nate glanced down at his sheet and all he'd have to do if he did come out on top. Was there any "winner" here? People from previous rounds... Did they really feel like winners after doing all they were made to do? It wasn't like the company got in touch with them afterwards to check up on them and see how they were doing. They were made to play the game, they were given the money once they had finished and then they were kicked to the curb. The company didn't give a shit about anyone.

Nate felt his heart skip a single beat as that nagging little voice came back to mind: *You think they give a shit about you? They're planning something. You fucked up. You cost them money and... They know everything. They're playing you and taking you for a fool. Just get up and go. Walk out of that door and keep walking. You only have one more question before you can leave. Those are the rules.*

Erica asked, 'How much to eat a stillborn baby?'

'Okay, no...' Mae got up and stormed from the room. Before she slammed the door she shouted, 'You're all fucking sick!'

Erica smiled. She knew that would be one that cleared people. They were fine doing all the disgusting stuff but - dead babies was always a step too far. The less people in the room after question ten, the less paperwork she needed to go through to work out the winner. She looked at the remaining contestants. When she locked eyes with Tracy she also stood up. Still smiling, Erica watched as the woman collected her coat from the back of her chair.

'If you could be quicker,' Erica said.

Tracy slowly walked to the front of the room and up to where Erica was getting impatient. She spat directly into Erica's face and said, 'You can have that one for free.'

'Get the fuck out of my room,' Erica said as she wiped the spit away from her cheek. Tracy laughed as she left. 'Cunt.'

Nate tried to stifle his smile but failed. Erica noticed.

Carol stood up and, in a more dignified manner, left the room. Only Nate remained with Miranda, the woman who'd previously been frustrated with the lack of speed in getting through the questions. She wasn't smiling either. She was staring dead ahead, a clear determination to leave the room as victor. The money was too important for her to leave a "loser".

Erica addressed them, 'And then there were two.'

They watched her as Erica pulled a seat out from close to one of the tables. She dragged it to the front of the room and turned it to face Miranda and Nate. She sat.

'Have you thought about what you would spend the money on?' Erica directed the question at Miranda.

'Can we just get on with the final question?'

'We're not in a rush.' Erica added, 'We like to know what our money is being spent on. After all, it wouldn't be very good if we found out you were funding some kind of terrorist organisation, would it?'

'I'm not funding any organisations.'

'Then you won't mind sharing with us what you're doing with the money?' Erica folded her arms. She wanted an answer, just because she was nosy and not for any other reason.

Miranda diverted the question across to Nate, 'What about him?'

Erica smiled. 'Well, he's not playing for money.'

'What?' Miranda didn't understand. 'What do you mean?' She asked him, 'You're doing this for fun?'

'I'm doing this for work,' Nate said. Nate turned to Erica and asked a question of his own, 'What are you doing?'

'Killing time. We have time. There's only two of you so there's not much paperwork to go through… The way the game is structured now… It takes a little longer to set up so…' She added, 'I'm just killing time.' She turned back to Miranda, 'What would you spend the money on?'

Miranda said nothing. It wasn't their business. She hadn't agreed to divulge what the money would be spent on and neither had they said she would need to. The way she saw it now, they could shut up and pay up.

Erica shrugged. 'Okay then, question number 10…'

'How much to put the remains of that stillborn baby back into its mother?'

Both Nate and Miranda looked at Erica. Both were equally as shocked although Nate should have known better. Of course it would be sick. That was the whole point.

'You know the rules. Both stayed for the final question so both have to see it through now…'

Miranda scribbled a number down. Nate hesitated. He had not realised, when he signed the contract for the job, that he had been signing his soul away to the Devil. He sighed and put a figure down. Unlike previous figures though, this one was *much* higher. Fuck the game, fuck the job and fuck them.

She'll leave you.

You'll lose the house.

You'll lose everything.

Nate didn't care anymore. It just wasn't worth any of this. It hadn't been from the moment he had been called into Sharon's office. In reality, it hadn't been from the moment he'd first gone for the fucking job. Time to call it a day.

'Okay, if you would like to pass me your papers… We will take a short break while we determine who is going through to the next stage.' Erica showed zero emotion as both Miranda and Nate handed their sheets over. With the pages in hand, she walked from the room, closing the door behind her.

Miranda couldn't help but to press Nate, 'What did you mean you're doing this for work?'

'You're playing a game of *How Much To* for money. I'm doing it to keep my job but, you know what, I don't want it. I don't want any of this anymore. I tried to change things but… I fucked up and… Well… Let's just say - congratulations.'

'Congratulations?'

'There's no way you bid higher than the figure I just put down.' He laughed. *One billion pounds to push the remains of a stillborn baby back into its mother.*

'My sister has cancer.'

'I'm sorry?'

'No insurance. I want to buy her private healthcare. Even if the doctors are saying there's no chance to beat it - I want to try and I want her to be comfortable in the best possible hospitals. That's what some of the money would go on. After that, I guess I'll clear my debts. They mounted over the years due to just being stupid with money…' She sighed. 'There's a lot I would fix and not just in my world…'

Nate gave her a sympathetic look. In an ideal world, this stranger would be able to do all of these things but not by going down this particular, unpleasant path. *His method had been better*. Or rather, it would have been "better" had it actually worked.

They both sat there a moment, in silence. It wasn't long before the door opened and Erica came back in with a case in hand. She took centre stage at the front of the room and set the case down on the chair she'd previously been sitting on.

'Well there is a very clear winner. Before we get to that though, I would like to let you into a *new* version of the game we will be playing. The winner here will be going up against another winner from a previous session. They had the same questions so don't worry. All is fair. The idea of the new game is to get through a series of rooms. Each one is set up with one of the questions you just answered… If you get through the rooms faster than the person you're competing against - you will get *double* the money you have bid for.'

'What the fuck is this?'

Erica laughed. '*This* is how you change the game to bring in more revenue and more viewers. Just think… People tune in to see who wins. People bet on who will win… Money comes pouring in… *You* wanted to change the game to make it better… Well, now you get a chance to be a part of that.'

Miranda asked, 'He won then?'

'No, darling, you did. But…' Erica opened the case up and pulled out a gun. She admitted, 'The game is rigged. Sorry.'

Before anyone could say or do anything, Erica pulled the trigger. The bullet fired through the air and penetrated Miranda's forehead. It ripped through her brain and obliterated the back of her head splashing fragments of brain and skull over the table and seats behind her own. As smoke billowed from the barrel of the gun and Nate jumped up in shock, Miranda's body slumped to the table.

'What the fuck are you doing?'

Erica lowered the gun and casually stated again, 'I'm rigging the game. *This* game was always going to be rigged but that's not the best bit. Want to meet the person you're playing against?'

'What are you even talking about anymore?'

Erica shouted, 'Okay…' Her word wasn't for Nate's benefit. It was for her colleague outside the room. They were standing there with the other runner.

Nate turned to the door as it opened, curious to see who he would be running against. His heart sank when a suited gentleman walked in, pushing Kim Spencer out in front of them. Kim had tears running down her cheeks.

The voice in his head whispered, *They know* _*everything*_*. I said that. I told you. They're playing you and now you're fucked.*

Chapter Ten

Erica was sitting with Nate. He had been forced to put on an orange jumpsuit. In a room nearby, Kim was wearing the same as the two were being prepared to compete.

'This is only the bare bones of how things are going to work. For the full picture, you need to imagine a host... Like a gameshow host. They'll be there, talking to a live studio audience, egging them on and getting them to bet... You know... Filling in the dead time while you two struggle to complete the tasks. No one wants dead time. It's boring. Keep things moving forward, keep things exciting and you keep people watching. *This* show is going to be one of the most watched online.' She paused a moment. Her expression changed from excitement to confusion. She asked, 'Why did you do it? Why did you not only try and change the formula but... Why did you *fake* it?'

'You wouldn't understand.'

'Try me.'

'Don't you get tired of watching people in desperate situations do these things? They don't deserve what we're doing to them. They're just trying to get on with their lives. What we do… What *you* are doing… It scars them. It breaks them… If they even survive in the first place.'

'So you thought you would - what? - make a little film and pretend it was real? You spent the company's money on that little shit show… Did you not think they watched the payments leaving their account? Do you not think that we ourselves are watched too?'

'I just wanted to help someone without spilling blood. What if my film had worked? What if the audience had lapped it up?'

'What about it?'

'We could fake everything and the viewers would never know the difference. Hell, go on the forums… Some people think we fake it all anyway… So what harm is there in faking it for real but paying off the people who played? An actor's fee for a job well done.'

'There's enough fake shit in the world…'

'There's even more horror in the world.'

Erica smiled. It was clear the two of them had very different outlooks on things now.

Erica's phone went off in her jacket pocket. She pulled it out and answered it. On the other end of the line, a voice said that they were ready. She hung the call up and slipped the phone back in her pocket.

'You ready to play the new game?'

'Do I get a choice?'

She laughed. 'Not really. Oh, one thing. Just to be clear. You're not playing for the money obviously. And, with the way things have gone, you're not playing for your job either.'

'Then why am I doing this?'

'Now you're playing for your freedom. Whoever completes the tasks the fastest gets to live.'

'They'll just open the door and release one of us? I'm supposed to believe that?'

'Well that's up to you but if you don't play, they'll kill you for viewing figures anyway so... Might as well see it through, right?'

Nate knew he had been backed into a corner with no other options. Reluctantly, he stood up. Erica led the way to the closed door. She knocked on it with a clenched hand and - from the other side - a woman unlocked it for them. Erica pulled the door open and froze.

'One more question?'

'I think I've had enough of these questions now.'

'It's an easy one, I promise.' Without waiting for his go ahead, Erica asked, 'How much to trade places with someone else?'

'Could it be you? I'd *pay* a lot of money...'

Erica laughed. 'Too bad you're broke, huh.' She stepped into the corridor. Nate followed.

PART THREE

THE GAME

Chapter Eleven

Kim stepped into the first room. It was a modest sized room with a table in the middle of it. A clear wall of unbreakable glass split the room (and table) in two and Nate was standing on the other side of it. One room had been turned to *his* and *her* room.

'I'm sorry,' he said.

She couldn't hear him through the see-through wall but she was able to understand what he'd said. She didn't respond. Instead she turned to the table. On both ends of the table there was a block of lard on a plate. One block each.

Kim recalled the rules. *Don't start until the light turns green.* She looked across to the other side of the room. Both Nate and Kim had another door to go through. No doubt, she presumed, it led through to the next challenge. Above the door though, important for now, there was a red light. Next to that there were two other bulbs; neither of which were illuminated. Before she had a chance to take anything else in, the second bulb lit. *Amber*. Similar to English traffic lights: Red, red-amber, green. Go on green.

The first two bulbs went out. The last lit up green.

Kim didn't rush for the block of lard, and neither did Nate. They both looked at the table and then at one another with neither of them really knowing what they wanted to do.

Kim turned back to the door she'd been pushed through. She wondered if the armed man was still standing out there or whether she could just leave the same way she had entered. Her unspoken question was answered when the door suddenly opened, along with the door on Nate's side too. In both doorways, men stood with guns. Each in turn cocked their weapon in a gesture meant as a threat: *Start playing or die.*

Nate looked up to the camera on the ceiling. Erica's words came back to mind, *Because we don't want you ruining the game for anyone, the sound won't be recorded this time but, when we play for real, we will get picture and sound for the viewers!* No point in shouting up to the camera that the whole thing was a fix if they couldn't hear. Even then, if he had tried, he'd probably just end up with a bullet lodged in the back of his spine anyway. He noticed Kim had walked over to the table and had the block of lard in her hand. She looked suitably disgusted, not that he could blame her. With another glance at the gun-man over his shoulder, he made his way to the table too. Neither of them seemed in a hurry to get from this room to the next.

He picked the lard up and sniffed it. Weirdly it didn't have much of a scent to it but he had a horrible feeling that wouldn't be the case when it came to the taste.

Kim was watching him, waiting for him to take the first bite. She wanted to gauge his reaction as to how bad it would be. He looked to be in no hurry to take that first bite.

Kim gave up waiting as she realised, the faster she got this done, the faster she could go back home. She closed her eyes, opened her mouth and bit down into the lard. It was fairly soft, no doubt because of how long it had probably been sitting out for. Kim kept her eyes closed as she bit down into another mouthful. The lard squelched between her teeth in the process whilst Nate watched on, wondering what was going through the woman's mind. *Did she know the rest of the tasks or had she just been thrown in here?*

When he noticed she was almost through it, swirling the mush around in her mouth before swallowing chunks at a time, he quickly started to eat too. Same story. The lard pushed up between his teeth and stuck to the room of his mouth with each bite. He didn't gag though and neither did she. Sure, it wasn't pleasant but - in the great scheme of things, it wasn't *too* bad. But Nate, at least, knew that this was only the first room.

Erica's voice suddenly came over the intercom, 'Okay you're both doing well but remember, this is a race. If you want to be let out, you really need to win this. But anyway, I need to talk about the next room... Nate, you know what was asked of you in the next room. You needed to suck on Audra's used tampon...'

Kim momentarily stopped eating the lard. Her eyes went wide with shock. It was in this moment that Nate realised Kim had no idea what was coming in the other rooms. The way she had looked at him earlier, when he had tried to apologise; it was safe to say she hadn't accepted his apology and that was *before* she knew what she was really involved in.

'Obviously there is only one of her and two of you so we have had to improvise for the next bit and discard the product Audra gave us. But, the principle and the game is the same as you'll see when you finish the lard.'

Because Kim had momentarily stopped, Nate was the first to finish eating. Immediately the next door automatically opened. The next room was shrouded in blackness. Slowly, he started to make his way across the room as Kim watched, hurriedly finishing her own block of lard. With the mouthful complete, her next door also opened.

Nate was first to step in. As he did so, the room lit up.

'What the fuck...'

The next room was the same in that it had a clear divide down the centre of it. Whereas the first room had a table within the divide, this one had a dead, naked woman built into it. She had been installed into the wall in a seated position with her chest, hands, feet, face and pussy on one side of the wall. Her back, including her buttocks and arsehole, was on the other side. Pieces of string were hanging from both her arse and her vagina.

When Nate walked up to the body, he instantly recognised the face. It was Miranda, the girl who *should* have won and been standing here.

Kim screamed as she stepped into the room and saw what was waiting. She looked away from the body only to see a sign on the wall which instructed her what needed to be done: *Remove and suck.*

Through the clear divide, she watched as Nate pulled on the string hanging from the dead woman's front. He held up a dirty tampon and, without giving it too much thought, quickly put it in his mouth and sucked hard on it.

The tampon had fresh blood on it. Some of it had even clotted, giving it a resemblance of blackcurrant jam, even though Nate knew it wasn't that. He didn't know if it was genuine period blood from the deceased woman though. Maybe it was? Maybe they killed her and, as luck would have it, she had been on her period? Or maybe they got the blood from another person?

Why are you even thinking about this?

Nate sucked harder still before - on the far wall - the next door unlocked and slowly opened. He immediately spat out the tampon, where upon it splattered onto the floor with a heavy, wet noise. He spat out for a second time; this time dispensing all of the *juice* and saliva that had collected in his mouth.

Kim turned her attention to the string hanging on her side of the body. Not that she wanted to, she gave it a pull. The tampon within slipped out easily, coated in a bile-yellow colour and followed with a trickle of liquid-shit. She retched but, at the same time, knew she didn't have time to mess around. Again, she closed her eyes. Then she brought the tampon up to her mouth. The smell hit instantly. An eggy-yeast mixture.

Don't think about it.

Nate was yelling out in pain from the next room. She focused on that, wondering what the hell was happening, and put the *lolly-pop (that's all it was)* into her mouth before she sucked it clean, gagging violently in the process. The door to the next room unlocked.

Nate was standing in the middle of the room. The usual barrier divided the two sides of the room but, this time, there was a concrete bar through the middle of it. The bar covered the entire length of the room with both ends imbedded into the walls on their respective sides. Nate's teeth were clamped over the bar on his side and he was moving his head along the length of the bar and back again in quick, short, hard movements. The motion caused a vibration through his head as he screamed through the pain of shaving his teeth down in uneven splinters.

Nate continued working the bar as Kim slowly made her way over to it. With horror in her eyes, she looked over to Nate. He stopped a moment. He had tears running down his face and blood dribbling down his chin. He turned back to the concrete and cried out in muffled pain as he bit down on the slab for a second time. His nerves already shot through thanks to his first effort at grinding his teeth down. He had known that it was going to hurt but, he had started so now he had to finish.

Nate dragged his mouth across it once more. His front tooth immediately snapped back in the gum and caused him to cry out again.

The next door in his room unlocked and slowly opened. With his eyes closed, Nate didn't realise and continued grinding down his broken, fractured pegs.

Kim opened her mouth wide and slowly bit down on the concrete. She gently applied pressure as she tested the "water". She pulled back, 'I can't do this.' She looked over, through to the other side of the room, to Nate's open door. He had seen it now and was stumbling towards it, holding his bloody mouth in pain.

'I can't do this,' she said. She screamed out in frustration only to then pull herself together. *She had to do this or the door would never open. At least, it would never open to freedom.*

Chapter Twelve

How Much To Fuck Yourself With A Dildo?

The question had been simple on paper. Nate put his number down as zero and suspected most of the others had done the same. A room full of women, most of them had probably, at one point, experimented with such a scenario. If anything, it was harder for him - a man. A woman fucks herself with a dildo? It's more or less the same as taking a dick. Their bodies were designed for such an occasion. For a man to fuck himself with a dildo, he would only have the one option and that was to go up the back passage. Sure there was a sweet spot up there to hit but, a good number of straight males would still not contemplate experimenting with such an area for risk of being perceived as gay.

Nate had never cared whether people thought of him as a homosexual or not. He certainly didn't have anything against them either. It was their life to live as they chose, just as his life was to live as he saw fit. That being said, he never felt the desire to test himself by inserting a finger, or a small toy. He was happy enough with "normal" sex: Prick in pussy. He liked the feeling, he got off on it. But - with the question raised as to how much he would need to fuck himself with a dildo? Well, nothing. He'd do it, he'd move on and maybe with a new bedroom trick to help get him off in those moments when a climax seemed to be just out of reach. Never say never.

Only now was he realising how foolish he had been to think that the question was as simple as it appeared. The dildo was eight inches in length so it wasn't ridiculous. It was made of rubber, it had make-shift veins up it to appear as a normal prick would, although the colour purple took away from the realism. Had that been all there was to it, then the task would have been simple. Hell, they had even provided a small tube of lubricant for the pair of them; one each. A nice gesture. Especially given how the dildo was wrapped in barbed-wire.

The sign on the wall reminded him of what to do in a simple, eloquent message: *Fuck Yourself Until It Ejaculates.*

As Kim screamed from the other room, Nate approached the dildo with apprehension. He really *was* going to "fuck" himself with this. There were balls attached to the toy and when he picked it up, he could feel watery movement from inside.

Blood ran from his mouth. Soon enough, blood would be running from another orifice and whilst the prospect didn't fill him with joy, and the pain was already substantial, he just wanted to get it over with. He wanted to get the whole damned thing over with.

Kim stumbled into the other side of the room. Her mouth had been obliterated and she had blood streaming too, along with tears running down her cheeks. Her complexion was both sweaty and pale; a shadow of her former self. She caught Nate's eyes. He still looked sorry for putting her in this position. She still hated him. She turned away and looked to what waited for her in the room. Despite the pain, when she read the note and saw the toy, she started to laugh. *Of course it would be something like this.*

Kim staggered towards the sex aid. She grabbed it from where it rested and took it towards the far wall where she slumped down to the floor. Nate watched. He still hadn't taken his toy.

Kim stared at him as she unbuttoned her orange jumpsuit. She pulled it down from her shoulders and pushed it down to her lower legs, exposing her top half and her white panties. With all she'd been through already, she felt no shame in Nate seeing how they had been stained, caused by the fear she had experienced after being snatched from the life she'd been living before they came for her. The hatred for that man - for Nate - who had put her in this position had overcome all fear and pain. Only one of them could survive? *She* wanted to survive. She wanted to win so that she could go home to her family. She wanted Nate to be stuck here forever… To go through whatever they had planned for the loser of the two.

She mouthed to him, 'Fuck you.' And, with that, she pulled her panties to one side and then started stabbing the adapted toy into her. As the barbs caught her labia and ripped them, she couldn't help but to scream as the first of the blood started to run freely. At no point did she take her eyes from Nate.

Nate watched for a moment and then realised he was wasting time. He unbuttoned his jumpsuit and lowered it down his body until his buttocks were exposed. A quick squirt into his hand with the provided lube and his smeared it into his arse. He squirted another load over the toy and then positioned it up against his virgin arsehole. Kim's toy, meanwhile, was deep inside her - ripping her up internally as she continued to scream and fuck herself as hard as she could.

Nate dropped to his knees and hovered over the toy. From here, it was easier to lower himself down to let his hole first get a taste of it and then to swallow it. He winced as it nudged against his ring. The feeling of the head pushing against him felt alien and, as a little more disappeared inside, it stung. He knew the pain would get worse... He saw Kim scream even louder on the other side of the sound-proof divide. Her face contorted in a way which suggested the pain was to get *a lot* worse.

Her next door unlocked as vinegar dribbled out of her destroyed cunt. Her labia hung in ripped tatters of flesh, dribbling blood. She dropped the toy to one side as she tried to get up to her feet. With her insides on fire as the vinegar mixed with her internal cuts, the pain was so intense that it was all she could do to crawl her way to the door.

Nate let out a scream as the first of the barbs dug into his skin and ripped its way towards his arsehole… *The pain was going to get so much worse.*

Once this room was finished, there'd still be six to go.

Chapter Thirteen

The next room had a number of screens hanging on the walls. On each of the screens, there was video footage playing of people shaving their verrucas over dinner plates. Some of the cameras recording them had macro lenses fitted so some screens showed the whole picture and others showed the flakes of skin coming away in close-up detail. Flaking away, peppering the plate. The plates themselves didn't just have verruca skin though. There were also long, yellow toenails - some crusted in toe cheese.

Between two of the screens, there was a sign with the words printed upon it stating: *Eat up.*

Nate crawled through to the room. On the other side, Kim was lying on the floor. She didn't move, having passed out from pain. It was all Nate could do to stay conscious himself. His arse was bleeding profusely, as was his mouth but he tried not to think of it as he looked at the screens hanging on the wall. From there, he looked to the table. Half of the table was on his side of the room. Half was on Kim's side. Both sides had a plate each and - on those... Flakes of hard, discoloured skin and human nails. Nate retched violently at the thought of eating it. No sick came up though, only blood which he promptly spat onto the floor.

Nate looked back over to Kim. He felt guilty for her being here and it didn't make him feel good now that she had passed out but, he had come so far and suffered so much. If she couldn't hack it then... He wasn't going to wait for her. Having come so far, he *couldn't* wait for her. He crawled towards the table with every little movement sending a bolt of pain through his body, coming from his rectum.

When he was close enough, Nate reached up to the plate. He brought it down to the floor and set it down. He gagged again as the smell of sweat and *cheese* hit him.

Cheese.

That's all it was. Just a fancy cheese purchased over the counter in a rich man's supermarket. Cheese. That's it.

He scraped the plate's contents into the palm of his other hand and held it there a moment, foolishly looking at it.

Cheese.

He opened his mouth, tipped his head back and palmed the flakes in. He immediately swallowed; not just the flakes of skin and clumps of nails but a mouthful of claret too from his shredded gums. He felt the sharpness of the nails claw their way down his food-pipe, after scratching the back of his throat. His stomach immediately grumbled in complaint at both the blood and skin peelings. Some of the latter had stuck to his broken and jagged teeth (the stumps that remained at least), coating them in what appeared to be a thin film. Only now was Nate thankful for the strong taste of blood in his mouth. Had it not been for that, he was sure the taste would have been horrific.

Small mercies.

The next door opened just as Kim started to come back around. Nate gave her a final look and then pushed forward, crawling through on all fours - still unable to walk.

Kim rolled onto her side and looked towards the screens, taking in all that was being displayed.

'Why are you doing this to me?' Her voice didn't sound like her anymore. The damage done to her mouth had completely contorted her voice so that she didn't recognise herself anymore. It didn't stop her from asking the watching cameras again, 'Why are you doing this to me?' It was a question she would never get an answer to. Her eyes welled.

*

How Much To Lick The Wall From One End To The Other? Again, a simple enough question. Take an average sized room. Now, how much would you take to lick the wall from one end to the other? Of all the tasks, the easiest - on paper at least. Kneeling in the room now, bleeding into his jumpsuit, Nate could see it wasn't the hardest of tasks but certainly wasn't the most unpleasant. At least, not in terms of *this* game.

More screens hung from the wall but there weren't people attending to their verrucas on these. Instead there were videos of people - young and old - picking their noses. Fingers buried deep in their nostrils, twisting and turning and then coming out with a string of snot sticking to them and a greenish-coloured lump of slime clinging to their finger-tip…

Along the wall, from one end to the other, there were a number of bogies stuck in place from the people in the video. A sign, at the far end of the wall detailed what needed to be done; lick the bogies off the wall, collect them on your tongue and then spit them into the tube in the far corner of the room. Once the weight was enough; the door would unlock.

Nate felt his stomach turn even though he knew, this was *easy* compared to what it could have been. They *could* have had a razor blade imbedded into the wall… This was definitely the better option. "The better option"? What the fuck was this game doing to him?

With some effort, Nate pulled himself up, using the wall to help steady him. He opened his mouth and poked his tongue out, ignoring his mouth-pain. Slowly, with trepidation, he tongue-fucked the first of the dried out greenies from the wall. Despite the dryness, it still tasted salty. Because of the dryness, it wasn't easy to get off the wall though.

Nate pulled a face so that one good tooth from the bottom row of teeth was jutted out front. An unnatural position; his jaw was already starting to ache. He scraped away the first of the wall's many deposits as, on the other side of the room, Kim appeared. She looked around at the screens, saw the sign and then looked through the clear divide to what Nate was doing. Had he been watching her, he would have seen her stomach visibly turn over.

From up above, the cameras in the ceiling continued to record their actions, broadcasting for all to see. Both Nate and Kim were working the walls.

The first few clumps of dried snot weren't too bad. Salty? Yes. But that was it. Had they been fresher and wetter then it would have been worse. As it was, it just felt like having salty flakes on the tongue as, other than the salt, there wasn't much else taste to be had; not that either of the couple were actively trying to taste it.

The biggest issue was the weight of a single bit upon the tongue. It felt light. Some of the bogies felt as though they added literally *nothing* to the weight already there. And, that meant, it would potentially take *a lot* of collecting to open the door.

Nate turned away from the wall and took his *collection* over to the tube close to the wall. With a healthy mixture of bloody saliva, he dribbled the first of the green debris into the tube. The door remained locked.

'Fuck.'

Kim wasn't just using a similar method to Nate. She was using her fingertips too. A little extra help to scrape the wall clean. *There was nothing in the rules.* When he saw what she was doing, Nate gave himself the extra help too; scraping the walls with both tooth and fingernails. Whatever was collected through, under the nail, was then scraped off onto the tooth and licked back onto the tongue. *Definitely an easier, and quicker, method.*

Adrenaline surged through both of their bodies which gave them the luxury of not feeling the previous pain that had plagued them. They moved fast and quick, desperate to get through to the end of this nightmare.

Kim dribbled her collection into the tube. Saliva, blood, clumps and lumps of bogey. The door lock clicked and the door opened into the next room; a room full of photographs. Nothing more and nothing less.

Kim glanced through to Nate. He was headed for his tube. Knowing she didn't have much of a head-start, she stepped into the next room. The door automatically closed behind her.

Kim stood there a moment, confused. Photographs? A sign that read: *Enjoy the memories for a moment.* Nothing more than that. But, despite how it might have looked, this was not a break. This was only going to make things much, much harder in the room after.

Nate's door opened and he stepped in. He looked mentally exhausted. *If only he knew what was to come.* Just as Kim was standing there with a look of confusion, a similar expression fell upon his face too.

'What the fuck is this?'

He looked at the first of the picture. The subject of each shot was the same as the last and that familiar, and unpleasant, sense of dread washed over him as though he were standing in a cold shower of emotion. This room was supposed to be about punching a child in the face. How much money would you take to hit a kid? It was fuck all to do with that though. The idea behind that question had clearly been substituted and the contents of this room linked directly to what he remembered of the following question.

Both Kim and Nate's heart skipped a beat as the door to the next door clicked open.

Chapter Fourteen

Nate knew what was waiting for him in the next room. He envied Kim's ignorance, not that she would be unaware for long as she made her way towards the open door.

He looked back at one of the photos stuck to the wall. It was him taken by his partner on a sunny day down the beach. He was sitting on a grassy embankment with his arm around the back of a Golden Labrador. Both were looking to the camera. He was smiling and even the Lab had an expression which resembled a smile as it sat there with its tongue hanging lazily from the side of its mouth.

Nate turned his attention to the camera on the ceiling. With hate in his eyes he warned them, 'If I make it out of here first, I'm going to kill you if you make me do this...' He remembered what they had said about the lack of sound but he *hoped* they'd be able to read his lips at least, even though the blood and general mess he'd made back in the concrete block room. He repeated again, slower this time, 'I… will… kill… you.'

Thanks to the divide between the rooms, he didn't hear Kim screaming, 'No!'

Slowly, he walked into the next room. Just as he worried, his pet dog Bernie was sitting there, tied to a little stake poking from the ground. On Kim's side of the room, she too was with one of her dogs; the animal they had pretended to previously kill for the video.

Bernie barked and instantly stood up the moment he saw Nate standing there, in the doorway. His tail wagged back and forth immediately as he moved as close to his master as the lead around his neck permitted. He barked again.

Nate stepped fully into the room with his eyes already welling up.

'Hello, boy…'

He moved closer to his beloved pet and dropped to his knees, wincing in pain from his internal tears in the process. Bernie didn't know he was hurt. He was just pleased to see him and stepped up onto Nate's lap, pushing his body against Nate's as close as he could get.

Nate couldn't help but laugh as Bernie started to lick his face. *Little kisses hello.*

Nate didn't want to look at the sign on the far wall and he did his best to ignore the knife, visible out of the corner of his eye. For now, he just wanted to enjoy Bernie's company.

'You're acting like you haven't seen me for ages,' Nate said despite only seeing each other that morning, before Nate left for work. 'Stupid boy,' he said with a laugh.

The little voice whispered back into his head, *What if he knows what you have to do? What if he is just trying to tell you how much he loves you?*

Nate tried to push the voice from his mind. He didn't want to think about it. He didn't want to hear it. He just wanted to enjoy this moment and hope that - actually - it was just a sick game and he didn't have to go through with it.

That was the problem though. It *was* a sick game and it was because of that, he *knew* he would have to do it. He closed his eyes and put his arms around Bernie's neck. This big, dumb dog had been the one happy constant in Nate's life from the day he had picked him up from the rescue centre. How someone could have abandoned a pup was beyond Nate. It was something he could never get his head around but, whatever their reason, he was grateful they had. Clearly they were undeserving of such a loving animal.

Whenever Nate was upset, it was Bernie who would make him smile. Whenever he was stressed, the dog would idly come by and just plop his head in Nate's lap. It was a move which prompted Nate to then start to pet him and, once he started petting Bernie… It was a move which helped take away the day's stress.

And now Bernie was perhaps the source of the most pain Nate would (and could) ever feel. He opened his eyes and looked up to the camera to those watching. He hated them. All of them. He hated the people who had put him there, he despised those who were sat in their comfortable homes or offices watching. Everyone who had any part in this show's creation were just scum.

Nate turned his head to the side but carried on holding his dog. Now he could see Kim through the clear divide. Her dog was desperately trying to get her attention. Its tail was wagging crazily too. Kim was on her knees, bent over with her head pressed to the floor and Nate could see her screaming. He could see the wetness of her tear-drenched cheeks. He had put her there and he felt that strong twist of guilt in his stomach. He had put her there by trying to be clever and beating the game to get people the money but letting them get away without having to experience any of the horrors demanded. He had set this up and now... This is what she had got. He knew he would never be forgiven. He knew he never deserved to be. It didn't stop him from being sorry though.

Nate took a deep breath and looked forward, past Bernie and to the sign: *Behead your own pet and put its head on the scales to unlock the door.* Nate felt sick. The original question, back in the classroom, had been

How much to kill an animal? Had it been *this*, most would have walked from the room, if not all of them. He certainly would have left, he knew that much for sure.

Close to the sign, there was a large, sharp kitchen knife. That was the weapon of choice. Next to the knife, there was a slot in the wall and another sign: *Put the knife through here when done*. Of course, they'd want that to be posted through. Had he been allowed to keep it, he would have used it on them the moment he got out of there.

Get out of there? How can he leave now? He turned back to Kim who'd moved to where the knife was. She had taken it back to her dog. Her dog was oblivious to what was to happen. It just wanted to be cuddled by its "mummy". Nate's gut twisted again.

An idea sprung to Nate's mind: If the door was activated by the scales, maybe he just needed to apply pressure to them in order to get the door to open? As quickly as his battered body would allow him, he stumbled over to the scales with Bernie following, desperate for his attention.

'Wait a minute,' Nate said.

He knelt on the floor - the most comfortable position for him - and started applying various amounts of weight to the scale by pushing down on them. Each time, there was a loud *buzz* noise, signifying the incorrect weight had been applied. He stopped and looked up at the camera. The doors weren't controlled by the scales at all. The scales were there for show only. The door was controlled by one of the company's employees, sitting there with a fucking coffee in their hand as they watched the proceedings.

'FUCK YOU!' Nate screamed up to the camera unaware that, on the other side of the divide, Kim had set the knife to her wrist instead.

Kim couldn't face going home and, unlike Nate, she had no idea how many more rooms she had to endure and what was to be found in them. For all she knew, the next room would have her kill her husband. The rooms after that? She'd have to kill her children and then - only then - would the final door open up to reveal the freedom she'd been promised *if* she won the race. But if that was the case, what had she won? If she was first forced to kill one of her pets and then her family - what was she going home to exactly? A life, potentially deformed, unable to cope with the heavy burden of guilt weighing down upon her. That wasn't living.

She slumped back against the wall and slid down it until her arse was on the cold floor. Her dog came over and climbed onto her lap. Its tail wagging enthusiastically such was the joy of seeing Kim. Just as Bernie had licked Nate's face, so was Kim's dog greeting her in a similar fashion. With tears streaming down her face once more, she put an arm around the animal and pulled it closer to her still, resting her forehead on its.

'I can't do it,' she said. 'I could never do it.'

But Nate could.

Nate *had* to. He would cut his dog's head off. He'd put it on the fucking scales and post them their damned knife and he'd go through the last of the fucking rooms and when he got out... He'd kill each and every person who was responsible for putting him in here and making him do this. More than that, he would do it with a smile on his face.

He leaned back against the see-through divider and, knife in hand, pulled Bernie close to him with his other arm. Bernie responded by licking Nate's face again. *Kisses for daddy.*

Unbeknownst to Nate, on the other side of the room, Kim pressed the knife down hard into her wrists. With her eyes scrunched up tight, she pulled the blade down her vein, opening it up wide. Whilst she still had a little strength in her already weakening hand, blood gushing out, she did the same to her other wrist as her dog barked. She dropped the knife. Her arms, pissing blood over the floor, slumped to her side as she wept through the pain.

Nate closed his eyes. He couldn't watch what he needed to do. If he closed his eyes and just hacked and sawed and then moved over to the scales, head in hand, then he would never *see* what he'd done meaning it had never happened. He realised that probably wouldn't be the case. The guilt would eat him alive as would the pain of killing his best friend but - it was still better than having to see it happen. The problem was, with his eyes closed, he missed the light above his locked door turning from red to green. With Kim taking herself out of the game, the show-runners were just keen to get Nate through to the next room; the beginning of the end. With only one person playing, the race was already won and the dog didn't *have* to die. The people running the show weren't animals after all... And, besides, there had already been a fair few complaints being aired in the online forums. Fuck with people, fine. Don't fuck with the animals.

Nate dragged the serrated edge of the knife's blade across the dog's throat. The dog immediately yelped and struggled to get away from him. Nate gripped his arm harder around the dog, keeping it in place as it continued to struggle in vain. With his other hand, he started hacking back and forth, ignoring the blood running down his arm and spraying across the room. The whole time, his eyes remained shut. *If he doesn't see it, it hasn't happened. He'll get home and just imagine that the dog had run away...*

Nate screamed. Pain. Anguish. Hatred. *Revenge.*

Chapter Fifteen

Nate entered the second to last room with his eyes still firmly shut. He had done all that had been asked of him in the previous room completely blind. *It didn't happen if he didn't see it.* The blood running down his face and soaking into his clothes, he just imagined as being his own from injuries sustained in the other rooms. *Not from the room he had just been in.* To his relief, he heard the door close behind him, blocking out everything that had happened permanently. There'd be no more reminders of that moment. Cautiously he opened his eyes. There was just a box in this room, sealed with a lid. He glanced through to the other side of the room; Kim's side. She hadn't come through yet. With his eyes closed for the last act, he hadn't seen that she'd opted to take her own life instead of carrying it through. He didn't realise she wouldn't be chasing, trying to beat him through to the end. He just figured she was

stuck, unable to go through with it. He couldn't blame her for thinking like that. In an ideal world he would have figured another way around it but - he needed to do it. He needed to get to the end of the game first so that he could take all the pain suffered and give it back to those who put him here. That was all he cared about now: Revenge. Cold, hard, bloody revenge.

Determined just to get through it now, Nate staggered towards the box. Kim had a box waiting for her on her side too. He didn't need to lift the lid to know what was waiting for him within it. Still, the lift needed to come off. He flicked it off with his hand and peered inside. There it was again; that twisting of the gut as he struggled not to spew up his insides.

Inside the box there was a baby foetus.

Nate's heard sunk. It wasn't what any person needed to see, whether they liked children or not. He remembered the question: *How Much To Eat A Stillborn Baby?* Stillborn? This poor little bastard hadn't even been born yet. *And how much needed to be eaten?*

Nate was "pleased" to see they'd at least provided a pair of dentures along with the body; forward planning on behalf of the show-runners after making him and Kim both grind out their teeth.

With a shaking hand, Nate reached in and took out the dentures. He slipped them in his mouth and winced in pain as they came into contact with his broken teeth and pushed down into his bruised gums. The sign on the wall gave further instruction: *Get The Key From The Little One's Stomach And Unlock The Door*!

Nate didn't hesitate. He reached in and took the corpse, with one hand around its ankles, from within the box. With his other hand, he took a hold of the deceased infant's head and stretched the body wider - giving him more surface-area of the stomach to bite down upon. That was the most logical place into which they could have placed the key. It made sense to start there.

The plastic teeth bit into the soft flesh easier than he expected. No doubt easier because the baby hadn't been cooked long enough in the womb so, therefore, hadn't properly formed. With the second, deeper bite - Nate coughed as a mouthful of liquid fat ejaculated into his mouth. He spat it out and bit down for a third time as the camera above monitored his every movement.

After the fourth bite, and mouthful of flesh and underdeveloped organs, he looked down at the hole he had made. Much to his relief, a small silver key was visible. Given the reaction to this task, by some of the other potential contestants, Nate had found this one relatively easy. But then, maybe that was just because of everything else he had experienced to get to this point?

He took the key from the tiny gut, spat the dentures out, and dropped the rest of the body into the box. If memory served correctly, he'd be needing it in the final room.

Before he headed for the door lock, Nate glanced back to the other side of the room. Still no Kim. Poor woman. Had his last door been open still, he would have gone back and warned her that he was headed for the final room now. It was bad enough she was in this position because of him anyway. What if he made it through to the final room and only *then* did she do what was needed in *that* room? It would have been for nothing and she would have to live with that.

If he could have gone back and warned her that it was already over, he would have. No such joy though. There were no handles on the backs of the doors. Once you passed through them, you passed through them. There was no turning back. All he could do was hope that she was refusing to compete anymore. Even if they didn't release her; at least she would get to stay with… Nate stopped his train of thought. He had done the act with his eyes closed for a reason. If he didn't see it happen, it hadn't happened. If he didn't talk or think about it, it didn't happen.

Nate moved to the door and slid the key into the lock. He twisted it until it wouldn't turn further and, then, he pulled the door open.

He froze.

In the next room, Carmen was lying on a bed in the centre of his half of the room. The clear divide was blacked out now so he couldn't see who, or what, was on the other side of the room. She was unconscious with a sheet covering her body.

'Carmen?' Nate didn't move from the doorway. He just looked at his unconscious partner with fear racing through him. 'What...' He stopped a moment as the final question came back to mind: *How Much To Put The Remains Back Inside The Mother*? As realisation hit home hard, he slowly turned back to the foetus. He couldn't see it from where he was standing, only the box. But he knew it was there.

'It's a game. It's just a sick game... They wouldn't.'

But, again, that was the problem: It was a sick game and because of that very reason, they *would*. He hurried over to where Carmen lay, ignoring the pain in his anal passage, and - without a word - he pulled back the covering sheet.

His heart skipped a beat.

Her stomach had a fresh wound. Stitches ran from one side to the other. *They'd cut his baby out of her and served it up to him cold.* Shocked, he stumbled back and screamed as the sign on the far wall instructed him further: *Look Under The Bed For Useful Tools. Get The Baby Back In The Parent Using Whatever Means You Like.*

Nervously, he looked under the bed. True enough, there was a tray hidden there and on the trap there were some tweezers and some lubricant. Tweezers, he presumed, would undo the stitching if he chose to go back in via the wound they'd already created. Lubricant for if he chose the *other* way.

Carmen moaned; a noise which caused Nate's heart to skip another beat. She was alive. Of course she was. It wouldn't have been hard had she been dead. He watched in horror as she slowly opened her eyes. Despite the drugs in her, she recognised him and forced a half-smile.

'Where am I?'

He couldn't answer her. She didn't know what he did at work exactly. He always gave a bullshit answer and changed the subject. Now, not only would she see the truth for herself - once fully conscious - but she would see what it had cost them both too.

She frowned.

'What happened to your face?'

In the shock of seeing her here, he had momentarily forgotten about the state of his mouth when he forced a smile back to her. He turned away and said, 'Don't look at me.'

'What's going on? Where am I?'

It was only then that Nate knew there was no leaving this nightmare. Even if he did push in the remains of the baby; he had lost everything and there was no getting it back. He could get out of there but he would never get his revenge. Not for this. How could he get anywhere close to what they'd done to him?

'My stomach hurts...'

He could try though but - in order to get out of the room - he still had to go through with the last question: *How Much To Put The Baby Back In The Parent?*

He smiled. They had never specified *which* parent. If he ate the remains then - technically - the baby would still be inside "the parent" as they'd demanded. She would never forgive him for this but, it was better than forcing the dead child back into her. He could, at least, spare her from that.

With a plan formulating in his mind, he turned back to Carmen and said to her, 'There's something I need to do but, I'll be back soon and when I am… I'll explain everything.' He added, 'I just hope you can forgive me.'

Carmen heard his words but was still struggling against the effects of the drugs. She told him, 'I don't understand.'

'I love you,' he said, 'and I'm sorry.'

He leaned down and kissed her on the forehead before he turned back to the room with the small box. He walked through the door and slowly pushed it to, blocking Carmen's line of sight for what he was about to do.

Nate walked over to the box and peered down. It was a boy. He was going to have had a little boy. As tears ran from his eyes, he smiled.

'Hello, son.'

He picked the dentures back up and slid them back into his mouth with effort. Then, he licked his lips.

Chapter Sixteen

Erica was watching the television monitor as Nate chewed into his son, swallowing chunks down with each mouthful. On her face was a look of shock. In the corner of the room, one of her colleagues was being sick into the waste paper basket.

The door opened and Sharon walked in.

Erica asked, 'Did you see?'

'I've been watching.'

'And?'

'And - I'm suitably impressed.'

'So?'

'So you can have your pay-rise.' She continued, 'I do think we need to re-think things, with regards to where we get the contestants, but I do believe we're onto a winning formula. Just as you said, people have been placing bets and the viewing figures are certainly impressive.'

'Re-think where we get the contestants?'

'Watching what you came up with, there is no way people will agree to take part for *any* amount of money. So, we'll go back to the old ways.'

'Which were?'

Sharon laughed. 'There's a lot of homeless people out there. Each of them, looking for someplace warm to stay... We'll offer them a place to stay.'

Erica smiled. 'So, we're really going to do this?'

'Like I said, I think you're onto a winner with this way of playing. Although the title *How Much To* will need to change though.'

'It will?'

'Well - we can offer prizes for people who *do* win, to keep them happy but... It's not really a game of *How Much To* anymore, is it?'

'So what do you suggest?'

Sharon shrugged. 'We'll probably just stick with *The Game*. It's easy to remember. It has a ring to it and people will be able to discuss it in public without others knowing what they're really watching...' He mocked a man's voice, 'Hey, you see The Game last night?' Back to her own voice she said, 'They'd just sound like every other guy in a bar.'

Erica smiled again. 'I like it.'

'That, though… *That* is disgusting.' She pointed to the screen. Nate was eating his dead son's arm; holding it to his mouth like a chicken wing and ripping the flesh from it. 'When he's finished, put a bullet in both him and his partner and let's get this cleaned up and ready for the next game.'

'Consider it done,' Erica said as she turned her attention back to the screen. She muttered to herself, 'The Last Supper.'

Author Bio

Matt Shaw is the author of over 200 published works. As well as appearing in a number of anthologies, Matt's work has been translated into French, German, Korean and Japanese. His work has also been adapted into graphic novels and - more recently - film.

Having successfully crowdfunded a feature film, in 2018 Matt Shaw adapted his best-selling novel MONSTER into a screenplay (with Shaun Hutson acting as script consultant) and then went on to direct it himself. The film starred Rod Glenn, Tracy Shaw (*Coronation Street)*, Laura Ellen Wilson and Danielle Harold (*Eastenders*). Having broken his "film cherry", Matt is currently producing two more feature films - one an original piece which he wrote for screen (*Next Door*) and a second based on another of his novellas (*Love Life*).

Matt tours both the UK and the US on regular book signings but - if you're unable to get to where he is - there is also a store where you can purchase signed merchandise direct from him over on ETSY. Simply look up *The Twisted World of Matt Shaw* where you'll find exclusive downloads, his infamous *DeadTed* bears and more…

Want to stay up to date with Matt? He can be found on Twitter, Instagram and Facebook. There is also a fan club which has exclusive stories, early reads, behind the scenes information and a whole lot more - available on Patreon!